GROOSHAM GRANGE

2 BOOKS IN 1!

Books by the same author

GROOSHAM GRANGE
and
RETURN TO
GROOSHAM GRANGE

Two Stories in One

ANTHONY HOROWITZ

WALKER BOOKS
AND SUBSIDIARIES

LONDON · BOSTON · SYDNEY · AUCKLAND

For Nicholas and Cassian

First published individually by Walker Books Ltd
87 Vauxhall Walk, London SE11 5HJ
as *Groosham Grange* (1995)
and *The Unholy Grail* (1999)

This edition published 2004

2 4 6 8 10 9 7 5 3

Text © 1988, 1999 Anthony Horowitz
Cover illustration © 2003 Phil Schramm

The right of Anthony Horowitz to be identified as author
of this work has been asserted by him in accordance with
the Copyright, Designs and Patents Act 1988

This book has been typeset in Sabon

Printed and bound in Great Britain by
Bookmarque Ltd, Croydon, Surrey

British Library Cataloguing in Publication Data:
a catalogue record for this book is
available from the British Library

ISBN 1-84428-573-1

www.walkerbooks.co.uk

GROOSHAM GRANGE

What happens when, aged eight, you get sent to the grimmest, most gruesome boarding school in England? You end up writing *Groosham Grange* and its sequel *Return to Groosham Grange* (previously published as *The Unholy Grail*). These are two of Anthony's favourite children's books and unlike his own schooldays they're full of humour and excitement.

Anthony is a popular and prolific children's book writer. In 2003 he was delighted to win the Red House Children's Book Award because it is voted for entirely by children. *Stormbreaker* was shortlisted for the same award in 2000 and *Point Blanc* was shortlisted in 2001. He also writes extensively for TV, with programmes including *Midsomer Murders*, *Murder in Mind* and *Poirot*. His hugely popular Sunday night drama series *Foyle's War* won the Lew Grade Audience Award in 2003.

Anthony is currently working on a series of five fantasy novels for Walker Books. He describes these as "Alex Rider with devils and witches". He has also written the screenplay of the film of *Stormbreaker*, which is moving ever closer to production, and – after his successful tour of Australia in 2003 – he is planning a new adventure, set there, for the Diamond brothers: *The Radius of the Lost Shark*. He is married to the television producer Jill Green and lives in north London with his two sons, Nicholas and Cassian, and their dog, Yucky.

Groosham Grange
CONTENTS

Return to Groosham Grange
CONTENTS

GROOSHAM GRANGE

ANTHONY HOROWITZ

EXPELLED

It was dinner time at 3, Wiernotta Mews.

Mr and Mrs Eliot were sitting at the dinner table with their only son, David. The meal that night had begun with a large plate of raw cabbage with cheese sauce because Mr and Mrs Eliot never ate meat. The atmosphere in the room was distinctly chilly. That afternoon, the last day of the Christmas term, David had brought home his school report. It had not made pleasant reading.

"Eliot has not made progress," the maths teacher had written. "He can't divide or multiply and will, I fear, add up to very little."

"Woodwork?" the carpentry teacher had written. "I wish he would work!"

"If he stayed awake in class it would be a miracle," the religion teacher had complained.

"Very poor form," the form master had concluded.

"He'll never get ahead," the headmaster had agreed.

Mr Eliot had read all these comments with growing anger. First his face had gone red. Then his fingers had gone white. The veins in his neck had gone blue and his tongue had gone black. Mrs Eliot had been unsure whether to call a doctor or take a colour photograph, but in the end, and after several glasses of whisky, he had calmed down.

"When I was a boy," he moaned, "if my reports weren't first class, my father would lock me in a cupboard for a week without food. Once he chained me behind the car and drove up the M1 and that was only because I came second equal in Latin."

"Where did we go wrong?" Mrs Eliot sobbed, pulling at her mauve-tinted hair. "What will the neighbours say if they find out? They'll laugh at me! I'm ruined!"

"My father would have killed me if I'd had a report like this," Mr Eliot continued. "He'd have tied me down to the railway line and waited for the 11.05 from Charing Cross..."

"We could always pretend we haven't got a son," Mrs Eliot wailed. "We could say he's got a rare disease. We could say he fell off a cliff."

As you will have gathered from all this, Mr

and Mrs Eliot were not the best sort of parents you could hope to have. Edward Eliot was a small, fat, bald man with a bristling moustache and a wart on his neck. He was the head of a bank in the City of London. Eileen Eliot was about a foot taller than him, very thin with porcelain teeth and false eyelashes. The Eliots had been married for twenty-nine years and had seven children. David's six elder sisters had all left home. Three of them had married. Three of them had emigrated to New Zealand.

David had been sitting at the far end of the polished walnut table, eating a polished walnut, which was all he had been given. He was short for his age and also rather thin – this was probably the result of being brought up on a vegetarian diet without really liking vegetables. He had brown hair, green-blue eyes and freckles. David would have described himself as small and ugly. Girls found him cute, which in his mind was even worse.

For the last half-hour his parents had been talking as if he wasn't there. But as his mother served up the main course – leek and asparagus pie with grated carrot gravy – his father turned and stared at him with a twitching eye.

"David," he said. "Your mother and I have discussed your report and we are not pleased."

"We are not!" Mrs Eliot agreed, bursting into tears.

"And I have decided that something must be done. I tell you now, if your grandfather were still alive he'd have hung you upside down by your feet in the refrigerator. That's what he used to do to me if I so much as sneezed without asking permission! But I have decided to be a little less severe."

"That's right! Your father's an angel!" Mrs Eliot sniffed into her lace handkerchief.

"I have decided, as far as you are concerned, to cancel Christmas this year. There will be no stocking, no presents, no turkey and no snow."

"No snow?" Mrs Eliot queried.

"Not in our garden. If any falls, I shall have it removed. I have already torn December 25 out of my diary. This family will go from December 24 to December 26. However, we shall have two December 27s to make up for it."

"I don't understand," Mrs Eliot said.

"Don't interrupt, my precious," Mr Eliot said, hitting her with a spoon. "If it weren't for your mother," he went on, "I would also give you a sound beating. If you ask me, there's not enough caning in this house. I was caned every day when I was a child and it never did me any harm."

"It did do you a bit of harm," Mrs Eliot muttered in a low voice.

"Nonsense!" Mr Eliot pushed himself away from the table in his electric wheelchair. "It made me the man I am!"

"But, darling. You can't walk..."

"A small price to pay for perfect manners!"

He turned the motor on and rolled towards David with a soft, wheezy noise. "Well...?" he demanded. "What have you got to say?"

David took a deep breath. This was the moment he had been dreading all evening. "I can't go back," he said.

"Can't? Or won't?"

"Can't." David pulled a crumpled letter out of his pocket and handed it to his father. "I was going to tell you," he said. "I've been expelled."

"Expelled? Expelled!"

Edward Eliot sank into his wheelchair. His hand accidentally struck the controls and he shot backwards into the roaring flames in the fireplace. Meanwhile Eileen Eliot, who had been about to take a sip of wine, uttered a strangled shriek and spilt the whole glass down her dress.

"I didn't like it there anyway," David said. He wouldn't normally have dared mention it. But he was in so much trouble already that a little more could hardly hurt.

"Didn't like it?" his father screamed, pouring a jug of water over himself to put out the fire.

"Beton College is the best public school in the country! All the best people go to Beton. Your grandfather went to Beton. Your great-grandfather went to Beton twice he liked it so much. And you can sit there and tell me...!"

His hand found the carving knife and he might have thrown it at his only son had Mrs Eliot not thrown herself on to him first, taking six inches of stainless steel into her chest. "Why didn't you like it?" he rasped as she slid in a heap on to the carpet.

David swallowed. He'd already marked the door out of the corner of his eye. If things got really bad he might have to make a dash for the bedroom. "I thought it was silly," he said. "I didn't like having to say good morning to the teachers in Latin. I didn't like cleaning other boys' boots and wearing a top hat and tails and having to eat standing on one leg just because I was under thirteen. I didn't like not having any girls there. I thought that was weird. And I didn't like all the stupid rules. When I was expelled they cut my tie in half and painted my jacket yellow in front of the whole school..."

"But that's tradition!" Mr Eliot screeched. "That's what public schools are all about. I loved it at Beton. It didn't bother me that there were no girls. When I married your mother I didn't even know she was a girl. It took me ten years to find out!"

He reached down and plucked the carving knife out of Mrs Eliot, then used it to tear open the letter. He read:

Dear Mr Eliot,

I very much regret to have to tell you that I have been forced to expel your son, David, for constant and wilful socialism.

Quid te exempta iuvat spinis de pluribus una?

Yours sincerely,

The Headmaster,
Beton College

"What does it say?" Mrs Eliot moaned as she slowly picked herself up from the floor.

"Socialism!" In two trembling hands Mr Eliot was holding the letter which suddenly separated as he tore it in half, his elbow catching his wife in the eye.

"I don't want to go to public school," David said miserably. "I want to go to an ordinary school with ordinary people and—"

It was as far as he got. His father had pushed the controls of the wheelchair to fast forward and was even now hurtling towards him with the carving knife while his mother screamed in pain. It seemed that he had just driven over her. David made a bolt for the door, reached it and slammed it shut behind him.

"If I'd talked to my father like that he'd have made me drink a gallon of petrol and then..."

That was all he heard. He reached his bedroom and threw himself on to his bed. Downstairs he could just make out the clatter of breaking dinner plates and the muffled shouts of his parents as they blamed each other for what had happened.

It was over. It hadn't even been as bad as he had expected. But lying alone in the gloom of his bedroom, David couldn't help wondering if there wasn't going to be worse to come.

THE PROSPECTUS

By the following morning a little sanity had returned to the Eliot household and although David had not dared leave the safety of his bedroom yet, his parents were sitting down at the breakfast table almost as if nothing had happened.

"Are you feeling better today, my little bowl of nuts, oats, dried fruit and whole wheat flakes?" Mrs Eliot enquired tenderly.

"We are not a muesli," Mr Eliot replied, helping himself to some. "How is the stab wound, my dear?"

"Not too painful, thank you, my love."

They ate their cereal in silence. As usual Mr Eliot read the *Financial Times* from cover to cover, clicking his teeth, sniffing and occasionally giggling as he found out which of his clients had gone bankrupt that day. On the other side of the table, Mrs Eliot, in a bright pink dressing-gown with matching hair curlers, hid behind the *Daily Mail* and slipped a little vodka into her cereal bowl. She liked a breakfast with schnapps, crackle and pop.

It was only when they had begun their boiled eggs that they remembered David. Mr Eliot had just bashed his egg with a teaspoon when his eyes glazed over and his moustache quivered.

"David..." he snarled.

"Do you want me to call him?" Mrs Eliot asked.

"What are we going to do with him?" Mr Eliot hammered at the egg again – too hard this time. The egg exploded, showering his wife with shell. With a loud sigh he threw down the spoon and tapped the *Financial Times*. "I had always hoped he would follow me into banking," he said. "That's why I bought him a pocket calculator when he was seven and a briefcase when he was eight. Every Christmas now for ten years I've been taking him to the Stock Market as a special treat. And what thanks have I got for it, eh? Expelled!" Mr Eliot grabbed hold of the *Financial Times* and tore it into a dozen pieces. "Washed up! Finished!"

Just then there was a clatter from the hallway as the post arrived. Mrs Eliot got up and went to see what had arrived but her husband went on talking anyway.

"If only I could find a school that could lick him into shape," he muttered. "Not one of these namby-pamby modern places but somewhere that still believes in discipline. When I was young, I knew what discipline meant! These days, most children can't even spell it. Whip, whip, whip! That's what they need! A good bit of bamboo on their bums!"

Mrs Eliot walked back into the breakfast room holding the usual bundle of bills and also a large brown envelope.

"Groosham Grange..." she said in a puzzled voice.

"What?"

"That's what it says on here." She held out the brown envelope. "It's postmarked Norfolk."

Mr Eliot snatched up a knife and Mrs Eliot dived behind the table, believing he was going to use it on her again. Instead he slit open the envelope before pulling out the contents.

"Strange..." he muttered.

"What is it, my dearest?" Mrs Eliot asked nervously over the edge of the table.

"It's a prospectus ... for a boy's school." Mr Eliot wheeled himself closer to the window where the sun was streaming in. "But how could anyone have known that we'd be looking for a new school for David?"

"Perhaps Beton College told them?" his wife suggested.

"I suppose so."

Mr Eliot opened the prospectus and a letter slid out. He unfolded it and read out loud.

Dear Mr Eliot,

Have you ever wondered where you could find a school that could lick your son into shape? Not one of those namby-pamby modern places but somewhere that still believes in discipline? And has it ever worried you that these days most children can't even spell discipline?

Mr Eliot lowered the letter. "Good heavens!" he said. "That's remarkable!"

"What is?" Mrs Eliot asked.

"I was saying exactly the same thing only a moment ago! Almost word for word!"

"Go on."

Mr Eliot picked up the letter.

Then allow us to introduce you to Groosham Grange. As you will see from the enclosed prospectus, we are a full boarding school and provide a unique environment for children aged twelve to sixteen who have proved themselves unsuited to modern teaching methods.

Groosham Grange is situated on its own island off the coast of Norfolk. There is no regular ferry service to the island so there are no regular holidays. In fact pupils are permitted only one day's holiday a year. Parents are never invited to the school except in special circumstances – and only if they can swim.

I feel confident that your son will benefit from the excellent facilities and high teaching standards of Groosham Grange. I look forward to hearing from you in the next half-hour.

Yours sincerely,

J Kilgraw

John Kilgraw
Assistant Headmaster

"Half-hour?" Mrs Eliot said. "That doesn't give us very long to make up our minds!"

"Mine's already made up!" Mr Eliot snapped. "Only one day's holiday a year! That's a sound idea if ever I heard one." He flicked through the prospectus which, curiously, contained no photographs and was written in red ink on some sort of parchment. "Listen to this! They teach everything ... with a special emphasis on chemistry, ancient history and religious studies. They have two language laboratories, a computer room, a fully equipped gymnasium and they're the only private school in the country with their own cemetery!" He tapped the page excitedly. "They have classes in drama, music, cookery, model-making ... and they've even got a class in astronomy."

"What would they want to have a class in a monastery for?" Mrs Eliot asked.

"I said astronomy – the study of the stars you ridiculous woman!" Mr Eliot rolled up the prospectus and hit her with it. "This is the best thing that's happened all week," he went on. "Get me a telephone."

There was a number at the bottom of the letter and Mr Eliot dialled it. There was a hiss, then a series of clicks. Mrs Eliot sighed. Her husband always hissed and clicked when he was excited. When he was in a really good mood he also whistled through his nose.

"Hello?" he said, once the connection had been made. "Can I speak to John Kilgraw?"

"This is Mr Kilgraw speaking." The voice was soft, almost a whisper. "I take it this is Mr Eliot?"

"Yes. Yes, it is. You're absolutely right!" Mr Eliot was amazed. "I got your prospectus this morning."

"And have you come to a decision?"

"Absolutely. I wish to enrol my son as soon as possible. Between you and me, Mr Kilgraw, David is a great disappointment to me. A massive disappointment. For many years I hoped he would follow in my footsteps – or at least in my wheelchair tracks, as I can't walk – but although he's almost thirteen he seems totally uninterested in merchant banking."

"Don't worry, Mr Eliot." The voice at the other end seemed to be devoid of emotion. "After a few terms at Groosham Grange I'm sure you'll find he's ... quite a different person."

"When can he start?" Mr Eliot asked.

"How about today?"

"Today?" Mrs Eliot was craning her neck to listen to the receiver. Mr Eliot swung it at her, catching her behind the ear. "I'm sorry, Mr Kilgraw," he said as she went flying. "That was just my wife's head. Did you say today?"

"Yes. There's a train leaving Liverpool Street for King's Lynn at one o'clock this afternoon. There will be two other pupils on it. David could travel with them."

"That's wonderful! Do you want me to come too?"

"Oh no, Mr Eliot." The assistant headmaster chuckled. "We don't encourage parents here at Groosham Grange. We find our pupils respond more quickly if they are completely removed from home and family. Of course, if you really want to make the long and tedious journey..."

"No! No! I'll just put him in a taxi to the station. On second thoughts, make that a bus."

"Then we'll look forward to seeing him this evening. Goodbye, Mr Eliot."

The phone went dead.

"They've accepted him!" Mr Eliot crowed. Mrs Eliot held the telephone out and he slammed the receiver down, accidentally crushing three of her fingers.

Just then the door opened and David came in, now wearing a T-shirt and jeans. Nervously he took his place at the table and reached out for the cereal packet. At the same time his father rocketed towards him and snatched it away, sending muesli in a shower over his shoulder. Mrs Eliot had meanwhile plunged her swollen fingers into the milk. David sighed. It looked as if he was going to have to give breakfast a miss.

"You don't have time to eat," Mr Eliot declared. "You've got to go upstairs and pack."

"Where am I going?" David asked.

"You're going to a wonderful school that I've found for you. A perfect school. A glorious school."

"But it's the end of term..." David began.

"The terms never end," his father replied. "That's what's so glorious about it. Pack your mother and kiss your clothes goodbye. No!" He banged his head against the table. "Kiss your mother and pack your clothes. Your train leaves at one."

David stared at his mother, who had begun to cry once again – though whether it was because he was leaving, because of the pain in her fingers or because she had somehow managed to get her hand jammed in the milk jug he could not say. There was obviously no point in arguing. The last time he'd tried arguing, his father had locked him in his bedroom and nailed up the door. It had taken two carpenters and the fire brigade a week to get it open again. Silently, he got up and walked out of the room.

It didn't take him long to pack. He had no uniform for the new school and no idea what books to take. He was neither happy nor particularly sad. After all, his father had already cancelled Christmas and whatever the school was like it could hardly be worse than Wiernotta Mews. But as he was folding his clothes he felt something strange. He was being watched. He was sure of it.

Closing his case, he walked over to the window and looked out. His bedroom had a view over the garden which was made entirely of plastic, as his mother was allergic to flowers. And there, standing in the middle of the plastic lawn, he saw it. It was a crow, or perhaps a raven. Whatever it was, it was the biggest bird he had ever seen. It was pitch-black, its feathers hanging off it like a tattered cloak. And it was staring up at the bedroom, its glistening eyes fixed on him.

David reached down to open the window. At the same moment, the bird uttered a ghastly, gurgling croak and launched itself into the air. David watched it fly away over the rooftops. Then he turned back and got ready to leave.

TRAVELLING COMPANIONS

David arrived at Liverpool Street Station at twelve o'clock. True to his word, his father had sent him on the bus. His mother hadn't come either. She had gone into hysterics on the doorstep and Mr Eliot had been forced to break a milk bottle over her head to calm her down. So David was quite alone as he dragged his suitcase across the forecourt and joined the queue to pick up his ticket.

It was a long queue – longer, in fact, than the trains everyone was waiting to get on. David had to wait more than twenty minutes before he reached a window and it was almost one o'clock before he was able to run for his train. A seat had been reserved for him – the school had arranged that – and he just had time to heave his case on to the luggage rack and sit down before the whistle went and the train began to move. Pressing his face against the glass, he stared out. Slowly the train picked up speed and London shuddered and rattled away. It had begun to rain. The scene could hardly have been more gloomy if he had been sitting in a hearse on the way to his own funeral.

Half an hour later they had travelled through the suburbs and the train was speeding past a number of dreary fields – all fields look much the same when they're seen through a train window, especially when the window is covered with half an inch of dust. David hadn't time to buy himself a book or a comic, and anyway his parents hadn't given him any money. Dejectedly, he slumped back in his seat and prepared to sit out the three hour journey to King's Lynn.

For the first time he noticed that there were two other people in the compartment, both the same age as him, both looking as fed up as he felt. One was a boy, plump, with circular wire-framed glasses. His trousers might have been the bottom of a school uniform. On top he was wearing a thick jersey made of so much wool that it looked as if the sheep might still be somewhere inside. He had long black hair that had been blown all over the place, as if he had just taken his head out of the washing machine. He was holding a half-eaten Mars bar, the toffee trailing over his fingers.

The other traveller was a girl. She had a round, rather boyish face with short brown hair and blue eyes. She was quite pretty in a way, David thought, or would have been if her clothes weren't quite so peculiar. The cardigan she was wearing could have belonged to her grandmother. Her trousers could have come from her brother. And wherever her coat had come from it should have gone back immediately, as it was several sizes too big for her. She was reading a magazine. David glanced at the cover and was surprised to see that it was *Cosmopolitan*. His mother wouldn't even allow *Cosmopolitan* in the house. She said she didn't approve of "these modern women", but then, of course, his mother was virtually prehistoric.

It was the girl who broke the silence. "I'm Jill," she said.

"I'm David."

"I'm J-J-Jeffrey." It was somehow not surprising that the fat boy had a stutter.

"I suppose you're off to this Ghastly Grange?" Jill asked, folding up the magazine.

"I think it's Groosham," David told her.

"I'm sure it will be gruesome," Jill agreed. "It's my fourth school in three years and it's the only one that doesn't have any holidays."

"W-w-one day a year," Jeffrey stammered.

"W-w-one day's going to be enough for me,"

Jill said. "The moment I arrive I'm heading out again."

"You'll swim away?" David asked. "It's on an island, remember."

"I'll swim all the way back to London if I have to," Jill declared.

Now that the ice had been broken, the three of them began to talk, each telling their own story to explain how they had ended up on a train bound for the Norfolk coast. David was first. He told them about Beton College, how he had been expelled and how his parents had received the news.

"I was also at p-p-public school," Jeffrey said. "And I was expelled too. I was c-c-caught smoking behind the cricket pavilion."

"Smoking is stupid," Jill said.

"It wasn't m-m-my fault. The school bully had just set fire to me." Jeffrey took off his glasses and wiped them on his sleeve. "I was always being b-b-bullied because I'm fat and I wear glasses and I've got a s-s-stutter."

Jeffrey's public school was called Godlesston. It was in the north of Scotland and his parents had sent him there in the hope of toughening him up. It had certainly been tough. Cold showers, twenty mile runs, porridge fourteen times a week – and that was just for the staff. At Godlesston, the pupils had been expected to do fifty press-ups before morning chapel and twenty-one more during it. The headmaster had come to classes wearing a leopard skin and the gym teacher had bicycled to the school every day, which was all the more remarkable as he lived in the Midlands.

Poor Jeffrey had been completely unable to keep up and for him the last day of term really had been the last. The morning after he had been expelled, his father had received a prospectus from Groosham Grange. The letter that went with it had been rather different from David's. It had made the school sound like a sports complex, a massage parlour and an army training camp all rolled into one.

"My dad also got a letter from them," Jill said. "But they told him that Groosham Grange was a really classy place. They said I'd learn table manners, and embroidery and all that sort of stuff."

Jill's father was a diplomat, working in South America. Her mother was an actress. Neither of them were ever at home and the only time she spoke to them was on the telephone. Once her mother had bumped into her in the street and had been unable to remember who she was. But like David's parents, they were determined to give her a good education and had sent her to no less than three private schools.

"I ran away from the first two," she explained. "The third was a sort of finishing school in Switzerland. I had to learn flower arranging and cookery, but I was hopeless. My flowers died before I could arrange them and I gave the cookery teacher food poisoning."

"What happened then?" David asked.

"The finishing school said they were finished with me. They sent me back home. That was when the letter arrived."

Jill's father had jumped at the opportunity. Actually, he had jumped on an aeroplane and gone back to South America. Her mother hadn't even come home. She'd just been given two parts in a Christmas pantomime – playing both halves of the horse – and she was too busy to care. Her German nanny had made all the arrangements without really understanding any of them. And that was that.

By the time they had finished telling their stories, David realized that they all had one thing in common. One way or another they were "difficult" children. But even so, they had no idea what to expect at Groosham Grange. In his parents' letter it had been described as old-fashioned, and for boys only. Jeffrey's parents had been told it was some sort of educational assault course. And Jill's parents thought they were sending their daughter to a posh ladies' college.

"They could be three completely different places," David said. "But it's the same school."

"And there's something else p-p-peculiar," Jeffrey added. "It's meant to be on an island next to N-N-Norfolk. But I looked on the map and there are no islands. Not one."

They thought about this for a while without speaking. The train had stopped at a station and there was a bustle in the corridor as people got on and off. Then David spoke.

"Listen," he said. "However bad this Groosham Grange is, at least we're all going there together. So we ought to make a pact. We'll stick together ... us against them."

"Like the Three M-M-Musketeers?" Jeffrey asked.

"Sort of. We won't tell anybody. It'll be like a secret society. And whatever happens, we'll always have two people we can trust."

"I'm still going to run away," Jill muttered.

"Maybe we'll go with you. At least we'll be able to help you."

"I'll lend you my swimming trunks," Jeffrey said.

Jill glanced at his bulging waist, thinking they would probably be more helpful if she used them in a parachute jump. But she kept the thought to herself. "All right," she agreed.

"Us against them."

"Us against th-th-them."

"Us against them." David held out his hand and the three of them shook.

Then the door of the compartment slid open and a young man looked in. The first thing David noticed was his dog-collar – he was a vicar. The second thing was that he was holding a guitar.

"Is that free?" he asked, nodding at one of the empty seats.

"Yes." David would have preferred to have lied. The last thing he needed right now was a singing vicar. But it was obvious that they were alone.

The young man came into the compartment, beaming at them in that horrible way that very religious people sometimes do. He didn't put his guitar up on the luggage rack but leant it against the opposite seat. He was in his thirties, with pink, rosy cheeks, fair hair, a beard and unusually bright teeth. As well as the dog-collar he was wearing a silver crucifix, a St Christopher medallion and a BAN THE BOMB sign.

"I'm Father Percival," he announced, as if anybody was slightly interested in who he was. "But you can call me Jimbo." David glanced at his watch and groaned silently. There were still at least two hours to King's Lynn and already the priest was working himself up as if any moment he was going to burst into song.

"So where are you kids off to?" he demanded. "Going on hols together? Or having a day out?"

"We're going to s-s-school," Jeffrey told him.

"School? Fab! Triffic!" The priest looked at them and suddenly realized that none of them thought it was at all fab or triffic. "Hey – cheer up!" he exclaimed. "Life's a great journey and it's first-class all the way when you're travelling with Jesus."

"I thought you said your name was Jimbo," Jill muttered.

"I'll tell you what," the vicar went on, ignoring her. "I know how to cheer you youngsters up." He picked up his guitar and twanged at the strings. They were horribly out of tune. "How about a few hymns? I made this one up myself. I call it 'Jesus, You're My Buddy' and it goes like this..."

In the hour that followed, Jimbo played six of his own compositions, followed by 'Onward Christian Soldiers', 'All Things Bright and Beautiful' and, because Christmas was approaching, a dozen carols. At last he stopped and rested his guitar on his knees. David held his breath, praying that the vicar wouldn't finish off with a sermon or, worse still, pass the collection plate around the carriage. But he seemed to have exhausted himself as well as them.

"So what are your names?" he asked.

Jill told him.

"Great! That's really super. Now tell me – Dave, Jeff and Jilly – you say you're off to school. What school's that?"

"Groosham Grange," David told him.

"Groosham Grange?" The vicar's mouth dropped open. In one second all the colour had drained out of his face. His eyes bulged and one of his cheeks, no longer rosy, twitched. "Groosham Grange?" he whispered. His whole body had begun to tremble. Slowly his fair hair rippled and then stood on end.

David stared at him. The man was terrified. David had never seen anyone quite so afraid. What had he said? He had only mentioned the school's name, but now the vicar was looking at him as if he were the devil himself.

"Grrooosss..." The vicar tried to say the words for a third time but they seemed to get caught on his lips and he hissed like a punctured balloon. His eyeballs were standing out like ping-pong balls now. His throat had gone dark mauve and it was evident from the way his body shuddered that he was no longer able to breathe.

"...ssss." The hiss died away. The vicar's hands, suddenly claws, jerked upwards, clutching at his heart. Then he collapsed, falling to the ground with a crash, a clatter and a twang.

"Oh dear," Jill said. "I think he's dead."

SKRULL ISLAND

The vicar had suffered a massive heart attack but he wasn't actually dead. The guard telephoned ahead, and at King's Lynn station a British Rail porter was standing by to whisk him away on a trolley to a waiting ambulance. David, Jill and Jeffrey were also met. One glance at the man who was looking out for them and they would have quite happily taken the ambulance.

He was horribly deformed. If he had been involved in a dreadful car crash and then fallen into an industrial mangle it could only have improved him. He was about five foot tall – or five foot short rather, for his head was closer to the ground than to his shoulders. This was partly due to the fact that his neck seemed to be broken, partly due to his hunched back. One of his eyes was several centimetres lower than the other and he had swollen cheeks and thin, straggly hair. He was dressed in a loose leather jacket and baggy trousers. People walking along the station were trying so hard not to look at him that one unfortunate woman accidentally fell off the platform. In truth it was hard to look at anything else. He was holding a placard that read GROOSHAM GRANGE. With a sinking heart, David approached him, Jeffrey and Jill following behind.

"My name is Gregor," he said. His voice came out as a throaty gurgle. "Did you have a good journey?"

David had to wait for him to say this again because it sounded like, "Dit yurgh av aghoot churnik?" When he understood, he nodded, lost for words. "Bring your bags then, young masters," Gregor gurgled. "The car is outside."

The car was a hearse.

It had been repainted with the name of the school on the side, but there could be no disguising the shape, the long, flat area in the back where its grisly contents should have lain. The people in the street weren't fooled either. They stopped in respectful silence, taking off their hats as the three children were whisked away towards their new school. David wondered if he wasn't in the middle of some terrible nightmare, if he wouldn't wake up at any moment to find himself in bed at Wiernotta Mews. Cautiously, he pinched himself. It had no effect. The hunchback hooted at a van and cursed. The hearse swept through a red light.

Gregor was a most peculiar chauffeur. Because of his height and the shape of his body, he could barely see over the steering wheel. To anyone out in the street it must have looked as if the car were driving itself. It was a miracle they didn't hit anybody. David, sitting in the front seat, found himself staring at the man and blushed when Gregor turned and grinned at him.

"You're wondering how I came to look like this, young master?" he declared. "I was born like it, born all revolting. I gave my mother the heebie-jeebies, I did. Poor mother! Poor Gregor!" He wrenched at the steering wheel and they swerved to avoid a traffic island. "When I was your age, I tried to get a job in a freak show," he went on. "But they said I was over-qualified. So I became the porter at Groosham Grange. I love Groosham Grange. You'll love Groosham Grange, young master. All the young masters love Groosham Grange."

They had left the city behind them now, following the coastal road up to the north. After that, David must have dozed off because the next thing he knew the sky had darkened and they seemed to be driving across the sea, the car pushing through the dark green waves. He rubbed his eyes and looked out of the window.

It wasn't the sea but a wide, flat field. The waves were grass, rippling in the wind. The field was empty but in the distance a great windmill rose up, the white panelled wood catching the last reflections of the evening sun. He shivered. Gregor had turned the heater on in the car but he could feel the desolation of the scene creeping in beneath the cushion of hot air.

Then he saw the sea itself. The road they were following – it was barely more than a track – led down to a twisted wooden jetty. A boat was waiting for them, half-hidden by the grass. It was an old fishing boat, held together by rust and lichen. Black smoke bubbled in the water beneath it. A pile of crates stood on the deck underneath a dirty net. A seagull circled in the air above it, sobbing quietly to itself. David hardly felt much better.

Gregor stopped the car. "We're here, young masters," he announced.

Taking their suitcases, they got out of the car and stood shivering in the breeze. David looked back at the way they had come but after a few twists and turns the road disappeared and he realized that they could have come from any-where. He was in a field somewhere in Norfolk with the North Sea ahead of him. But for the windmill he could have been in China for all the difference it would have made.

"Cheerful, isn't it," Jill said.

"Where are we?" David asked.

"God knows. The last town I saw was called Hunstanton, but that was half an hour ago." She pulled her cardigan round her shoulders. "I just hope we get there soon," she said.

"Why?"

"Because the sooner we arrive, the sooner I can run away."

A man had appeared, jumping down off the boat. He was wearing thigh-length boots and a fisherman's jersey. His face was almost completely hidden by a black beard, as black as the eyes which shone at them beneath a knotted mass of hair. A gold ring hung from his left ear. Give him a sword and an eye-patch and he could have walked straight out of *Treasure Island*.

"You're late, Gregor," he announced.

"The traffic was bad, Captain Bloodbath."

"Well, the tide is worse. These are treacherous waters, Gregor. Treacherous tides and treacherous winds." He spat in the direction of the sea. "And I've got a treacherous wife waiting for me to get home, so let's get moving." He untied a rope at the end of the jetty. "All aboard!" he shouted. "You ... boy! Weigh the anchor."

David did as he was told although the anchor weighed so much that he could hardly lift it. A moment later they were away, the engine coughing, spluttering and smoking – as indeed was Captain Bloodbath. Gregor stood beside him. The three children huddled together at the back of the boat. Jeffrey had gone an unpleasant shade of green.

"I'm not m-m-much of a sailor," he whispered.

The captain had overheard him. "Don't worry!" he chortled. "This ain't much of a boat!"

A mist had crept over the water. Now its ghostly white fingers stretched out for the boat, drawing it in. In an instant the sky had disappeared and every sound – the seagull, the engine, the chopping of the waves – seemed damp and distant. Then, as suddenly as it had come, it parted. And Skrull Island lay before them.

It was about two miles long and a mile wide with thick forest to the east. At the southern end, a cliff rose sharply out of the frothing water, chalk-white at the top but a sort of muddy orange below. A twist of land jutted out of the island, curving in front of the cliff, and it was to this point that Captain Bloodbath steered the boat. Another jetty had been built here and there was an open-top Jeep standing nearby. But there was no welcoming committee, no sign of the school.

"Stand by with the anchor!" the captain called out. Assuming he meant him, David took it. Bloodbath spun the wheel, slammed the engine into reverse and shouted. David dropped the anchor. Jeffrey was sick over the side.

They had arrived.

"This way, young masters. Not far now. Just a little more driving." Gregor was the first on land, capering ahead. Jeffrey followed, weakly dragging his suitcase. David paused, waiting for Jill. She was watching Captain Bloodbath, who was already raising the anchor, backing the boat out.

"What are you waiting for?" he asked.

"We may need that boat one day," Jill muttered. "I wonder if he ever leaves it."

"Captain Bloodbath..." David shivered. "That's a funny name."

"Yes. So how come I'm not laughing?" Jill turned round and trudged along the jetty to the Jeep.

It took them five minutes to reach the school. The track curved steeply upwards, rising to the level of the cliffs, then followed the edge of the wood. Jeffrey had grabbed the seat in the driving compartment next to Gregor. David and Jill were sitting in the back, clinging on for dear life. Every time the Jeep drove over a stone or a pot-hole – and there were plenty of both – they were thrown about a foot in the air, landing with a heavy bump. By the time they arrived, David knew what it must feel like to be a salad. But he quickly forgot his discomfort as he took in his first sight of Groosham Grange.

It was a huge building, taller than it was wide; a crazy mixture of battlements, barred windows, soaring towers, slanting grey slate roofs, grinning gargoyles and ugly brick chimneys. It was as if the architects of Westminster Abbey, Victoria Station and the Brixton gasworks had jumbled all their plans together and accidentally built the result. As the Jeep pulled up outside the front door (solid wood, studded with nails and sixteen inches thick) there was a rumble overhead and a fork of lightning crackled across the sky.

Somewhere a wolf howled.

Then the door creaked slowly open.

MR KILGRAW

A woman stood in the doorway. For a moment her face was a livid blue as the lightning flashed. Then she smiled and David saw that she was, after all, human. In fact, after the peculiar horrors of Gregor and Captain Bloodbath, she seemed reassuringly normal. She was small and plump, with round cheeks and grey hair tied in a bun. Her clothes were Victorian, her high collar fastened at the neck with a silver brooch. She was about sixty years old, her skin wrinkled, her eyes twinkling behind gold half-glasses. For a moment she reminded David of his grandmother. Then he noticed the slight moustache bristling on her upper lip and decided that she reminded him of his grandfather too.

"Hello! Hello!" she trilled as the three of them climbed down from the Jeep. "You must be David. And you're Jill and Jeffrey. Welcome to Groosham Grange!" She stood back to allow them to enter, then closed the door after them. "I'm Mrs Windergast," she went on. "The school matron. I hope the journey hasn't been too tiring?"

"I'm tired," Gregor said.

"I wasn't asking you, you disgusting creature," the matron snapped. "I was talking to these dear, dear children." She beamed at them. "Our new arrivals!"

David looked past her, taking in his surroundings. He was in a cavernous entrance hall, all wood panels and musty oil paintings. A wider staircase swept upwards, leading to a gloomy corridor. The hall was lit by a chandelier. But there were no lightbulbs. Instead, about a hundred candles spluttered and burned in brass holders, thick black smoke strangling what little light they gave.

"The others are already eating their evening meal," Mrs Windergast said. "I do hope you like blood pudding." She beamed at them for a second time, not giving them a chance to answer. "Now – leave your cases here, Jeffrey and Jill. You follow me, David. Mr Kilgraw wants to see you. It's the first door on the left."

"Why does he want to see me?" David asked.

"To welcome you, of course!" The matron seemed astonished by the question. "Mr Kilgraw is the assistant headmaster," she went on. "He likes to welcome all his new pupils personally. But one at a time. I expect he'll see the others tomorrow."

Jill glanced at David and shrugged. He understood what she was trying to tell him. Mrs Windergast might seem friendly enough but there was an edge to her voice that suggested it would be better not to argue. He watched as Jill and Jeffrey were led away across the hall and through an archway, then went over to the door that the matron had indicated. His mouth had gone dry and he wondered why.

"I expect it's because I'm terrified," he muttered to himself.

Then he knocked on the door.

A voice called out from inside and, taking a deep breath, David opened the door and went in. He found himself in a study lined with books on one side and pictures on the other with a full-length mirror in the middle. There was something very strange about the mirror. David noticed at once but he couldn't say exactly what it was. The glass had been cracked in one corner and the gilt frame was slightly warped. But it wasn't that. It was something else, something that made the hairs on the back of his neck stand up as if they wanted to climb out of his skin and get out of the room as fast as they could.

With an effort, he turned his eyes away. The furniture in the study was old and shabby. There was nothing strange about that. Teachers always seemed to surround themselves with old, shabby furniture – although the dust and the cobwebs were surely taking things a bit too far. Opposite the door, in front of a red velvet curtain, a man was sitting at a desk, reading a book. As David entered, he looked up, his face expressionless.

"Please sit down," he said.

It was impossible to say how old the man was. His skin was pale and somehow ageless, like a wax model. He was dressed in a plain black suit, with a white shirt and a black tie. As David sat down in front of the desk, the man closed the book with long, bony fingers. He was incredibly thin. His movements were slow and careful. It was as if one gust of wind, one cough, or one sneeze would shatter him into a hundred pieces.

"My name is Kilgraw," he continued. "I am very happy to see you at last, David. We are all happy that you have come to Groosham Grange."

David wasn't at all happy about it, but he said nothing.

"I congratulate you," Mr Kilgraw went on. "The school may seem unusual to you at first glance. It may even seem ... abnormal. But let me assure you, David, what we can teach you, what we can offer you is beyond your wildest dreams. Are you with me?"

"Yes, sir."

Mr Kilgraw smiled – if you could call a twitching lip and a glint of white teeth a smile. "Don't fight us, David," he said. "Try and understand us. We are different. But so are you. That is why you have been chosen. The seventh son of the seventh son. It makes you special, David. Just how special you will soon find out."

David nodded, searching for the door out of the corner of his eye. He hadn't understood anything Mr Kilgraw had said but it was obvious that the man was a complete nutcase. It was true that he had six elder sisters and six gruesome aunts (his father's sisters) who bought him unsuitable presents every Christmas and poked and prodded him as if he were made of Plasticine. But how did that make him special? And in what way had he been chosen? He would never have heard of Groosham Grange if he hadn't been expelled from Beton.

"Things will become clearer to you in due course," Mr Kilgraw said as if reading his mind. And in all probability he had read his mind. David would hardly have been surprised if the assistant headmaster had pulled off a mask and revealed that he came from the planet Venus. "But all that matters now is that you are here. You have arrived. You are where you were meant to be."

Mr Kilgraw stood up and moved round the desk. There was a second, black-covered book resting at the edge and next to it an old-fashioned quill pen. Licking his fingers, he opened it, then leafed through the pages. David glanced over the top of the desk. From what he could see, the book seemed to be a list of names, written in some sort of brown ink. Mr Kilgraw reached a blank page and picked up the quill.

"We have an old custom at Groosham Grange," he explained. "We ask our new pupils to sign their names in the school register. You and your two friends will bring the total up to sixty-five who are with us at present. That is five times thirteen, David. A very good number."

David had no idea why sixty-five should be any better than sixty-six or sixty-four, but he decided not to argue. Instead, he reached out for the quill. And it was then that it happened.

As David reached out, Mr Kilgraw jerked forward. The sharp nib of the quill jabbed into David's thumb, cutting him. He cried out and shoved his thumb into his mouth.

"I'm so sorry," Mr Kilgraw said. He didn't sound sorry at all. "Are you hurt? I can ask Mrs

Windergast to have a look at it, if you like."

"I'm all right." David was angry now. He didn't mind if Mr Kilgraw wanted to play some sort of game with him. But he hated being treated like a baby.

"In that case, perhaps you'd be so good as to sign your name." Mr Kilgraw held out his pen but now it was stained bright red with David's blood. "We won't need any ink," he remarked.

David took it. He looked for ink on the desk but there wasn't any. The assistant headmaster was leaning over him, breathing into his ear. Now all David wanted was to get out of there, to get something to eat and to go to bed. He signed his name, the nib scratching red lines across the coarse white paper.

"Excellent!" Mr Kilgraw took the pen and slid the book round. "You can go now, David. Mrs Windergast will be waiting for you outside."

David moved towards the door, but Mr Kilgraw stopped him. "I do want you to be happy here, David," he said. "We at Groosham Grange have your best interests at heart. We're here to help you. And once you accept that, I promise you, you'll never look back. Believe me."

David didn't believe him but he had no intention of arguing about it now. He went to the door as quickly as he could, forcing himself not to run. Because he had seen what was wrong with the mirror. He had seen it the moment after he had signed his name in blood, the moment he had turned away from the desk.

The mirror had reflected everything in the room. It had reflected the desk, the books, the curtains, the furniture, the carpet and David himself.

But it hadn't reflected Mr Kilgraw.

THE FIRST DAY

7.00 a.m.

Woke up with a bell jangling in my ear. The dormitory is high up in one of the school's towers. It is completely circular with the beds arranged like the numbers on the clock face. I'm at seven o'clock (which is also the time as I sit here writing this). Jeffrey is next to me at six o'clock. His pillow is on the floor, his sheets are all crumpled and he has somehow managed to tie his blanket in a knot. No sign of Jill. The girls all sleep in another wing.

7.30 a.m.

I am now washed and dressed. One of the boys showed me the way to the bathroom. He told me his name was William Rufus, which was a bit puzzling as I saw the name-tape on his pyjamas and it said James Stephens. I asked him why he was wearing somebody else's pyjamas but he just smiled as if he knew something that I didn't. I think he *does* know something I don't!

I don't think I like the boys at Groosham Grange. They're not stuck up like everyone at Beton College, but they are ... different. There was no talking after lights out. There was no pillow fight. Nothing. At Beton College every new boy was given an apple-pie bed – and they used real apple pies. Here, nobody seems at all interested in me. It's as if I weren't here at all (and I wish I weren't).

7.45 a.m.
Breakfast. Eggs and bacon. But the bacon was raw and the eggs certainly didn't come out of a chicken! I have lost my appetite.

9.30 a.m.
William Rufus – if that really is his name – took me to my first lesson. He is short and scrawny with a turned-up nose and baby-blue eyes. He was just the sort who would always have been bullied at Beton, but I don't think there is any bullying at Groosham Grange. Everyone is too polite. I don't believe I just wrote that! Whoever heard of a polite schoolboy?

William and I had a weird discussion on the

way to the classroom.

"It's double Latin," he said.

"I hate Latin," I remarked.

I thought we'd have at least one thing in common, but I was wrong. "You'll like it here," he told me. "It's taught by Mr Kilgraw and he's very good."

He looked at his watch. "We'd better hurry or we'll be late."

"What's the punishment for being late?" I asked.

"There are no punishments at Groosham Grange."

Good Latin teachers? A school with no punishments? Have I gone mad?

But double Latin wasn't as bad as it sounded. At Beton College it was taught as a "dead" language. And the teacher wasn't much healthier. But Mr Kilgraw spoke it fluently! So did everyone else! By the end of the lesson they were chatting like old friends and nobody even mentioned Caesar or the invasion of Gaul.

Another odd thing. It was a bright day, but Mr Kilgraw taught with the shutters closed and with a candle on his desk. I asked William Rufus about this.

"He doesn't like the sun," William said. At least, I think that's what he said. He was still talking in Latin.

11.00 a.m.

Saw Jill briefly in the break. Told her about this diary. She told me about her day so far. For some reason she's in a different class to Jeffrey and me.

"I had Mr Creer for modelling," she said.

"Pots?" I asked.

"Completely pots. We had to make figures out of wax. Men and women. And he used real hair."

Jill showed me her thumb. It was cut just like mine. She had seen Mr Kilgraw immediately after breakfast.

"I'm seeing him after lunch," Jeffrey said.

"Bring your own ink," Jill suggested.

12.30 p.m.

English with Miss Pedicure.

Miss Pedicure must be at least a hundred years old. She is half blind and completely bald. I think she's only held together by bandages. She seems to be wrapped up in them from head to toe. I could see them poking out of her sleeves and above her collar. It took her fifteen minutes to reach her chair and when she sat down she almost disappeared in a cloud of dust.

Miss Pedicure does have perfect teeth. The only trouble is, she keeps them in a glass on the corner of her desk.

She taught Shakespeare. From the way she talks, you'd think she knew him personally!

1.15 p.m.
Lunch. Mince. But what was the animal before it was minced? I think I am going to starve to death.

3.00 p.m.
I was meant to have French this afternoon but the teacher didn't show up. I asked William Rufus why.

WILLIAM: It must be a full moon tonight. Monsieur Leloup never teaches when there's going to be a full moon.

ME: Is he ill?

WILLIAM: Well, he isn't quite himself...

We all had books to read but I couldn't make head nor tail of them. I spent most of the lesson writing this, then examined the other kids in the class. I know most of their names now. Marion Grant – red-headed with freckles and big teeth. Bessie Dunlop – thin and pretty if you don't look too close. Roger Bacon – Hong Kong Chinese. Since when was Roger Bacon a Chinese name?

In fact all these names sound wrong. Bessie just doesn't look like a Bessie. Why is it that I think everyone is sharing some sort of horrible secret? And that Jeffrey, Jill and me are the only ones on the outside?

4.30 p.m.
Football. We played with an inflated pig's bladder. I scored a goal, but I didn't feel too good about it. You should try heading an inflated pig's bladder...

6.00 p.m.
We ate the rest of the pig for tea. It was turning on a spit with an apple in its mouth. At least I managed to grab the apple!

6.30 p.m.
I am back in Monsieur Leloup's classroom doing prep. That's what I'm supposed to be doing anyway. Instead I'm writing this. And I've just noticed something. I suppose I noticed it from the very start. But it's only just now that I've realized what it is.

Everyone in the class is wearing a ring. The same ring. It is a band of plain gold with a single black stone set in the top. What on earth does it mean? I've heard of school caps and school badges, but school rings?

I have re-read my first day's diary. It doesn't make a lot of sense. It's as if I've been seeing everything on a video recorder that's been fast forwarded. I get the pieces but not the whole picture.

But if I wrote down everything I'd end up

with a whole book. And something tells me I ought to leave time for my will.

7.30 p.m.
An hour's free time before bed. No sign of Jeffrey or Jill. Went for a walk in the fresh air.

The football field is at the back of the school. Next to it there's a forest – the thickest I've ever seen. It can't be very big but the trees look like a solid wall. There's a chapel at the back and also a small cemetery.

Saw Gregor sitting on a gravestone, smoking a cigarette. "Too many of those, Gregor," I said, "and you'll be under it!" This was a joke. Gregor did not laugh.

8.15 p.m.
Happened to see Jeffrey chatting to William Rufus. The two looked like the best of friends. Is this worrying?

8.40 p.m.
In bed. The lights go out in five minutes.

I had a bath this evening. The bathroom is antique. When you turn on the tap the water rushes out like the Niagara Falls, only muddier. Got out of the bath dirtier than when I went in. Next time I'll shower.

After I'd finished writing the last entry in this diary, I put it away in the cupboard beside the bed with a pencil to mark the place. When I got back, the diary was in exactly the same position, but the pencil had rolled out.

SOMEBODY READ THIS WHILE I WAS OUT OF THE ROOM!

So I won't be writing any more so long as I'm at Groosham Grange. I have a feeling it would be better to keep my thoughts to myself.

Questions:

Are all the names false? If so, why?

What is the meaning of the black rings?

What's really going on at Groosham Grange?

And don't worry, whoever's reading this. Somehow I'm going to find the answers.

IN THE DARK

Despite his resolution, David had learnt nothing by the end of the next day. The school routine had ticked on as normal – breakfast, Latin, history, break, maths, lunch, geography, football – except that none of it was remotely normal. It was as if everything, the lessons and the books, was just an elaborate charade, and that only when it was sure that nobody was looking the school would reveal itself in its true colours.

It was half past seven in the evening. David was working on an essay in the school library – a room that was unusual in itself in that it didn't have any books. Instead of bookshelves, the walls were lined with the heads of stuffed animals gazing out of wooden mounts with empty glass eyes. Not surprisingly, David hadn't found it very easy to concentrate on Elizabethan history with two moles, an armadillo and a wart-hog staring over his shoulder.

After twenty minutes, he gave up. He had no interest in the Spanish Armada and he suspected he could say the same for Miss Pedicure (who also taught history). He examined the page he had just finished. It was more ink-blots and crossing out than anything else. With a sigh he crumpled it in a ball and threw it at the dustbin. It missed and hit the large mirror behind it. David sighed again and went over to retrieve it. But it had gone. He searched behind the dustbin, under the chairs and all over the carpet in front of the mirror. But the ball of paper had vanished without trace. Suddenly, and for no good reason, David felt nervous. He glanced over his shoulder. The wart-hog seemed to be grinning at him. He hurried out of the library, slamming the door behind him.

A narrow, arched passageway led out from the library and back into the main hall. This was the passage he had come down on his first evening at Groosham Grange. It went past the door of Mr Kilgraw's study and now he paused outside it, remembering. That was when he heard the voices.

They were coming from the room opposite Mr Kilgraw's, a room with a dark panelled door and the single word HEADS painted in gold letters. So Groosham Grange had not one but two headmasters! David filed the knowledge away, puzzled that he hadn't yet seen either of them. He quickly looked about him. The other pupils had already left the library ahead of him. He was alone in the passage. Pretending to tie up his shoelace, he knelt beside the door.

"...settled in very well, I think." David recognized the voice at once. There could be no mistaking the dusty syllables of Mr Kilgraw. "The girl was a touch difficult in her modelling class, but I suppose that's only to be expected."

"But they all signed?" This was a high-pitched, half-strangled voice. David could imagine someone inside the room, struggling with a tie that was tied too tight.

"There was no problem, Mr Teagle." Mr Kilgraw laughed, a curiously melancholy sound. "Jeffrey – the boy with the stutter – came in last. He brought his own pencil. And two bottles of ink! In the end I had to hypnotize him, I'm afraid. After that, it was easy."

"You think this Jeffrey is going to be difficult?" This voice was the softest of the three. The second headmaster didn't speak so much as whisper.

"No, Mr Fitch," Mr Kilgraw replied. "If anything, he'll be the easiest. No. The one I'm worried about is Eliot."

"What's wrong with him?"

"I don't know for sure, Mr Teagle. But he has a certain strength, an independence..."

"That's just what we need."

"Of course. But even so..."

David was desperate to hear more of the conversation but just then Mrs Windergast appeared, walking towards the library. Seeing him, she stopped and blinked, her eyes flickering behind the half-glasses.

"Is there anything the matter, David?" she asked.

"No." David pointed feebly at his shoes. "I was just tying my lace."

"Very wise of you, my dear." She smiled at him. "We don't want you tripping over and breaking something, do we? But perhaps this isn't the place to do it – right outside the headmasters' study. Because somebody might think you were eavesdropping and that wouldn't be a very good impression to give in your first week, would it?"

"No," David agreed. He straightened up. "I'm sorry, Mrs Windergast."

He moved away as quickly as he could. The matron brushed past him and went into the headmasters' study. David would have given his right arm to have heard what they were saying now. But if he was found outside the door a second time, they would probably take it.

Instead he went in search of Jeffrey and Jill. He found them outside the staff room. Jill was examining the pigeon holes, each one labelled with the name of one of the teachers.

"Have you seen Monsieur Leloup's pigeon hole?" she asked, seeing him.

"What about it?"

"It's got a pigeon in it." She pointed at it, grimacing. The bird was obviously dead. "It looks like some wild animal got it."

"What's it doing there?" David asked.

"You'll have to ask Monsieur Leloup," Jill said.

"If he ever sh-sh-shows up," Jeffrey added.

Together they walked back down the corridor. One side was lined with lockers. The other opened into classrooms. A couple of boys passed them, making their way up to the dormitories. There was almost an hour until the bell went, but it seemed that most of the pupils of Groosham Grange had already gone to bed. As ever, the silence in the school would have been better suited to a museum or a monastery. In the entire day, David hadn't heard a door slam or a desk bang. What was going on at Groosham Grange?

They found an empty classroom and went into it. David hadn't been in this room yet and looked around him curiously. The walls were covered with posters showing various animals – inside and out. Instead of a desk, the teacher had a long marble slab which was covered with scientific apparatus: a burner, a small metal cauldron and various bottles of chemicals. At the far end, a white rat cowered in a cage and two toads stared unhappily out of a glass tank. The skeleton of some sort of animal stood in one corner.

"This must be the biology lab," David whispered.

"I wish it was," Jill shook her head. "All this stuff has been left out since my first class this afternoon."

"What c-c-class was that?" Jeffrey asked.

"Cookery."

David swallowed, remembering the mince.

Jill sat down behind one of the desks. "So let's compare notes," she said.

"Our first two days at Groosham Grange," David agreed.

"Jeffrey – you go first."

Jeffrey had little to say. He was the most miserable of the three of them, still confused after his meeting with Mr Kilgraw. He hadn't done any work at all and had spent the whole of the last lesson writing a letter to his mother, begging her to take him away. The only trouble was, of course, that there was nowhere to post it.

"I hate it here," he said. "It isn't t-t-tough like I thought it would be. But it isn't anything like I th-th-thought it would be. All the t-t-teachers are mad. And nobody's t-t-teased me about my stammer."

"I thought you didn't like being teased," David said.

"I d-d-don't. But it would be more n-n-normal if they did."

"Nothing's normal here," Jill broke in. "First of all they make us sign our names in blood. The lessons are like no lessons I've ever sat through. And then there's the business of the rings."

"I saw them too," David said.

"They're all wearing the same ring. Like some sort of bond."

"And I've found out more." David went on to describe his discoveries of the day, starting with the mystery of the pyjamas. "I may be wrong," he said, "but I get the feeling that everyone here is using false names."

"There's a boy in my class called Gideon Penman," Jill muttered.

"Exactly. What sort of a name is that?"

"B-b-but why would they have false names?" Jeffrey asked.

"And why do they want our real names in blood?" Jill added.

"I found out something about that too," David said and went on to describe the conversation outside the headmasters' study. He left out the bit about Jeffrey being the weakest of them mainly because he thought it would be cruel to mention it. But also because it was probably true. "All I can say is that the sooner we're out of here the better," he concluded. "There's something nasty going on at Groosham Grange. And if we stay here much longer I think it's going to happen to us."

Jeffrey looked accusingly at Jill. "I thought you were going to r-r-run away."

"I will." Jill glanced out of the window. "But not tonight. I think there's going to be another storm."

The storm broke a few minutes later. This time there was no lightning, but the cloudburst was spectacular nonetheless. It was as if the sea had risen up in a great tidal wave only to come crashing down on the school. At the same time, the wind whipped through it, tearing up the earth, punching into the brickwork. Loose shutters were ripped out of their frames. A gravestone exploded. A huge oak tree was snapped in half, its bare branches crashing into the soil.

It was the sound of the falling tree that woke David for the second time that day. Scrabbling in his bedside cabinet, he found his torch and flicked it on, directing the beam at his watch. It was just after midnight. He lay back against the pillow, gazing out of the window. There was a full moon; he could just make out its shape behind the curtain of rain. When he was a child, David had never been frightened by storms. So he was surprised to find that he was trembling now.

But it wasn't the weather. In the brief moment that the torch had been on, he had noticed something out of the corner of his eye, something that hadn't been fully registered in his mind. Sitting up again, he turned it back on, then swung the beam across the dormitory. Then he knew what it was.

Jeffrey was asleep in the bed next to him, his head buried underneath the covers. But otherwise the two of them were alone. When the lights had gone out at nine-thirty, the other boys in the dormitory had already been asleep. Now their beds were empty, the covers pulled back. He directed the torch on to their chairs. Their clothes had gone too.

Quietly, he slipped out of bed and put on his dressing-gown and slippers. Then he went to the door and opened it. There were no lights on in the school. And the silence was more profound, more frightening than ever.

He tried a second dormitory, then a third. In each one the story was the same. The beds were empty, the clothes were gone. Outside, the rain was still falling. He could hear it pattering against the windows. He looked at his watch again, certain that he was making some sort of crazy mistake. It was twenty past twelve. So where was everybody?

He could feel his heart tugging against his chest as if it were urging him to go back to bed and forget all about it. But David was wide awake now. He would get to the bottom of this even if it killed him. And, he thought to himself, in all probability it would.

He tiptoed down the corridor, wincing every time he stepped on a creaking floorboard. Eventually he reached a fourth dormitory. He shone the torch on the handle of the door.

Behind him, a hand reached out of the gloom. It settled on his shoulder.

David felt his stomach shrink to the size of a pea. He opened his mouth to scream and only managed to stop himself by shoving the torch between his teeth. It was a miracle he didn't swallow it. Slowly he turned round, the back of his neck glowing bright red with the beam of the torch shining through his throat.

Jill stood opposite him. Like him, she wearing a dressing-gown and slippers. She looked even more frightened than he did.

"Where are they?" she whispered. "Where have they gone?"

"Nggg..." David remembered the torch in his mouth and pulled it out. "I don't know," he said. "I was trying to find out."

"I saw them go." Jill sighed, relieved to have found David awake and out of bed. "It was about twenty minutes ago. One of them woke me up as she left the dormitory. I waited a bit and then followed them."

"So where did they go?" David asked, repeating Jill's own question.

"I saw them go into the library," Jill replied. "All of them. The whole school. I listened at the door for a bit but I couldn't hear anything, so then I went in myself. But they weren't there, David." Jill took a deep breath. David could see that she was close to tears. "They'd all vanished."

David thought back. He had been in the library after tea, surrounded by the stuffed animal heads. It was a small room, barely big enough for sixty-three people. Apart from a table, a mirror, a dozen chairs and the animals, there was nothing in it. And that included doors. There was only one way in. Only one way back out again.

"Maybe they've all gone outside?" he

suggested. "Through a window."

Jill scowled at him. "In this weather? Anyway, the windows in the library are too high. I know. I tried…"

"Then they must be somewhere in the school."

"No." Jill slumped against the wall, then slithered down to sit on the floor. She was exhausted – and not just through lack of sleep. "I've looked everywhere. In the classrooms, in the dining hall, in the staff room … everywhere. They're not here."

"They've got to be here somewhere!" David insisted. "They can't just have disappeared."

Jill made no answer. David sat down next to her and put an arm around her shoulders. Neither of them spoke. David's last words echoed in his thoughts. "They've got to be here somewhere! They can't just have disappeared."

But sitting in the dark and silent passage he knew that he was wrong.

Impossible though it seemed, they were alone in Groosham Grange.

CHRISTMAS

Three days before Christmas it began to snow.

By Christmas Day the whole island had been blanketed out. The ground was white. The sea was white. It was difficult to tell where one ended and the other began, and standing in the fields you felt like a single letter on a blank page in an envelope waiting to be posted.

There was no central heating at Groosham Grange. Instead, huge logs burned in open fire-places, crackling and hissing as if they were angry at having to share their warmth. All the windows had steamed up and the plumbing shuddered, groaned and gurgled as the water forced its way through half-frozen pipes. A colony of bats that inhabited one of the northern towers migrated downstairs for warmth and ended up in the dining-room. Nobody complained. But David found mealtimes something of a struggle with about a hundred eyes examining his rhubarb crumble upside down from the rafters.

Apart from the bats and the weather, nothing else had changed at the school. At first David had been surprised that nobody seemed to care about Christmas. Later on he had glumly accepted it. Captain Bloodbath came to the school once a week, on Tuesdays, but he never brought any letters or took any so there were no Christmas cards. There were no Christmas decorations either. David had seen Mrs Windergast with an armful of holly and that had raised his spirits – at least until lunchtime, when he had had his first taste of holly soup. There was no Christmas tree and, of course, no Christmas presents. Despite the snow, nobody threw any snowballs and the only snowman turned out to be Gregor, who had dozed off on his gravestone just before the heaviest fall and had to be thawed out the next day.

Only one teacher even mentioned Christmas, and this was Mr Creer in religious studies. Mr Creer was the only normal-looking teacher in the whole school. He was the youngest too, about thirty, short with curly hair and a neat moustache. His full name was Ronald Edward Creer. David had been a little unsettled to see the same name on a tombstone in the school cemetery – "Drowned off Skrull Island: 1955-1985" – but he had assumed it was a relative. Nonetheless, Mr Creer did smell very strongly of seaweed.

"Christmas, of course, has very little to do with Christianity." Mr Creer gave the class a ghostly smile. All his smiles were rather ghostly. "There were festivals at the end of December long before Christianity appeared; the Roman 'Saturnalia' and the Persian 'Birth of the Sun', for example. In the north it is a festival of the dark spirits, for it is at Christmas that the dead return from their graves."

This was all news to David. But he had to admit that living in London and being surrounded by tinsel, department-store Santas, last-minute shopping, mince pies, puddings and too many old films on TV, Christmas had never had much to do with Christianity there either.

Christmas Day began like any other day: baths, breakfast, three lessons, then lunch. For some reason, however, the lessons in the afternoon had been cancelled and David and Jill found themselves free to wander as they pleased. As usual, all the other pupils went to bed. That was what they did whenever they had any free time. Then, late at night, they would go to the library. And then they would disappear.

David and Jill had tried to follow them several times, determined to get to the bottom of the mystery, but without success. The trouble was that there was no way they could follow the others into the library without being seen, and by the time they opened the door everyone had gone. One afternoon they searched the room thoroughly, certain that there must be a secret passage. But if there was a secret passage, it must have had a spectacularly secret entrance. All the walls seemed to be made of solid brick. A fireplace with a stone mantelpiece dominated one of them, and there was a full-length mirror in a frame decorated with bronze flowers on the other. But though David pressed and prodded all the animals while Jill fiddled with the mirror and even tried to climb up the chimney, they didn't find anything.

And where was Jeffrey during all this?

In the weeks that they had been at Groosham Grange, Jeffrey had changed and this worried David more than anything. He still remembered Mr Kilgraw's words. "If anything, he'll be the easiest..." It was certainly true that Jeffrey had taken to spending more and more time by himself and less and less time with David and Jill. Quite a few times now, David had seen him in deep conversation with William Rufus and although he had questioned him about it, Jeffrey had refused to be drawn. Although there were no books in the library, he seemed to be reading a lot; old, dusty books with yellowing pages bound in cracked leather.

It was Jill, with her short temper, who had finally started an argument. She had rounded on him one evening in an empty classroom as they talked about their progress – or lack of it.

"What's wrong with you?" she demanded. "You're beginning to act as if you actually like it here!"

"Perhaps I d-d-do," Jeffrey replied.

"But the whole school is mad!"

"All p-p-public schools are mad. But it's a lot b-b-better than Godlesston."

"But what about our promise?" David reminded him. "Us against them."

"We may be ag-g-gainst them," Jeffrey said. "But I'm not so sure that they're ag-g-gainst us."

"Then why don't you just go off and join them?" Jill snapped.

It looked as if Jeffrey had.

David and Jill were alone as they trudged across the playing fields, up to their ankles in snow. They knew every inch of the island by now. Groosham Grange was in the north. A forest sprawled all the way down to the eastern side. Its trees could have been sculpted out of stone and looked at least a thousand years old. The point, where the jetty stood, was at the southernmost end. This was a long, flat area below the multicoloured cliffs which soared up behind. David was sure that he could see the entrance to a cave at the bottom of the cliffs and would have liked to explore it, but there was no way they could reach it. The cliffs themselves were too sheer to climb down and the point was separated from the cave by an inlet, the waves pounding at the rocks and sharpening them into needlepoints.

There was also a river on the island – although it was more of a wide stream – running from the north into a lake beside the forest. This was where they went to now. The water had frozen over and they had thought it would be fun to go skating. But they didn't have any skates. And anyway, they didn't feel much like having fun ... even if it was Christmas Day.

"Have you learnt anything since you got here?" Jill asked.

David considered. "Not really," he admitted. "But then there are never any tests or exams or anything so it doesn't really seem to matter."

"Well, I've learnt one thing." Jill picked up a stone and threw it across the lake. It hit the ice and slithered into a tangle of weeds. "The boat comes every Tuesday. Captain Bloodbath unloads all the supplies and then he and Gregor drive up to the school. So for about one hour there's nobody on the boat."

"What of it?" David asked, suddenly interested.

"The day after Boxing Day is a Tuesday. And when they're up at the school there is going to be somebody on the boat. Me."

"But there's nowhere to hide." David had been with Jill when she had examined the boat a week before. "We looked."

"There isn't room for two," Jill admitted. "But I reckon one of us can squeeze inside the cabin. There's a heap of old rags on the floor. I think I can hide underneath."

"So you're really going." David couldn't help feeling sad as he spoke the words. Jill was his only true friend in the school. With her gone, he would be more alone than ever.

"I've got to go, David," Jill said. "If I stay here much longer I'm going to go crazy ... like Jeffrey. But once I'm away, I'll send a letter to the authorities. They'll send someone over. And I bet you anything you like, the school will be closed down a week later."

"Where will you go?" David asked.

"I've got four brothers and two sisters to choose from," Jill said. She smiled. "We were a big family. I was number seven!"

"Did your mother have brothers and sisters?" David asked.

Jill looked at him curiously. "What on earth has that got to do with anything?"

"I just wondered..."

"As a matter of fact she was a number seven, too. I've got six uncles. Why do you want to know?"

"Seventh daughter of a seventh daughter," David muttered and said no more. It meant something. It had to mean something. But what?

He was still pondering over it later that evening as he sat by himself in the library. Christmas dinner – if you could call it that – had been ham and chips, the chips only slightly warmer than the ham. David was feeling really depressed for the first time since he had arrived. Jill had gone to bed early and there wasn't even any television to cheer him up. There was one television in the school but it was a black and white model held together by Sellotape. The volume switch had fallen off and the reception was so bad that the screen always resembled a miniature snowstorm. It was fine if you were watching a programme about deaf and dumb coal workers in Siberia. Otherwise it was useless.

The door opened and he looked up. It was Jeffrey.

"Hello," he said.

"Hello, D-D-David." The fat boy stood hovering beside the door as if he was embarrassed to have been caught there.

"I haven't seen you around for a while," David said, trying to sound friendly.

"I know. I've been b-b-busy." Jeffrey looked round the room, his eyes darting behind his wire-frame spectacles. "Actually, I w-w-was looking for W-W-William."

"Your new friend?" Now David sounded scornful. "Well, he's not here. Unless of course he's under the c-c-carpet or in the f-f-fireplace or wherever it is they all go at night! And all I can say is, if you want to join them, they're welcome to you."

"I d-d-didn't..." Jeffrey stammered to a halt, blushing, and David felt angry with himself for having lost his temper. He opened his mouth to speak again but at the same time Jeffrey backed out of the room, shutting the door behind him.

David got up. *He'll be the easiest.* Once again Mr Kilgraw's words echoed in his mind. Of course Jeffrey would be the easiest of the three of them – whatever it was that Groosham Grange had planned. He was fat. He wore glasses and he had a stutter. He was one of life's victims, always the one to be bullied. And by rejecting him, David had just played right into their hands. It had been three against the rest when they began. But his own thoughtlessness had left Jeffrey out there on his own.

84

Quickly, he left the library. Jeffrey had already disappeared down the corridor but David didn't mind. If he could find out what was really going on at Groosham Grange – behind the façade of the lessons and everyday school life – then perhaps he might be able to put a stop to it, saving Jeffrey and himself at the same time. And he was in the perfect place to start looking. The answer had to be in one of two rooms.

He began with the door marked HEADS. In all the time he had been at the school he had never once seen the two headmasters, Mr Fitch and Mr Teagle. But for the fact that he had heard their voices, he wouldn't have believed they even existed. Now he knocked gently on the door. As he had expected, there was no reply. Glancing over his shoulder, he reached for the handle and turned it. The door opened.

David had never been in the headmasters' study before. At first sight it reminded him more of a chapel than a study. The windows were made of stained glass showing scenes from what looked like the Last Judgement, with devils prodding naked men and women into the flames. The floor was made of black marble, and there was no carpet. The bookcases, filled with ancient books like the one Jeffrey had been reading, reminded him of pews and there was even a pulpit in one corner, a carved eagle supporting a Bible on its outstretched wings.

The room had one riddle of its own. There were two headmasters at Groosham Grange. So why was there only one desk, only one chair, only one gown on the clothes-stand behind the door? David could find no answer to that – and no answers to anything else. The desk drawers were locked and there were no papers lying around. He spent five fruitless minutes in the study. Then he left as quietly as he had gone in.

It took more courage to sneak into Mr Kilgraw's study opposite. David remembered the last time he had been there – he still had a mark on his thumb to show for it. Eventually he opened the door. "He can't eat you," he muttered to himself, and wished that he believed it.

There was no sign of the assistant headmaster but as he crossed the carpet, he felt he was being watched. He stopped, scarcely daring to breathe. He was quite alone in the room. He moved again. The eyes followed him. He stopped again. Then he realized what it was. The pictures...! They were portraits of grim old men, painted, it would seem, some years after they had died. But as David moved, their eyes moved with him so that wherever he was in the room they were always looking at him.

He paused beside what looked like a chest of

drawers and rested his hand against it. The wood vibrated underneath his fingertips. He pulled his hand away and stared at it. Had he imagined it? No – standing there alone in the study, he could hear a faint humming sound. And it was coming from the chest.

Squatting down, he reached for one of the drawers and pulled it. That was when he made his first discovery. The whole chest was a fake. All three drawers were no more than a front and swung open like a door. The chest was actually a modern refrigerator.

David peered inside and swallowed hard. The chest might be a fridge but it certainly didn't contain milk, butter and half a dozen eggs. Instead, about thirty plastic bags hung from hooks, each one filled with a dark red liquid. "It's wine," he whispered. "It's got to be wine. Of course it's wine. It can't be anything else. I mean, it can't be..."

Blood!

But even as he slammed the door and straightened up, he knew that it was. Wine didn't come in bags. Wine was never labelled AB POSITIVE. He didn't even want to ask what thirty pints of it were doing in Mr Kilgraw's study. He didn't want to know. He just wanted to get out of the study before he ended up in another eight bags on a lower shelf.

But before he had reached the door, he managed to stop himself. It was too late to back out now. This might be the last chance he had to search the study. And time was running out for Jeffrey. He took a deep breath. There was nobody around. Nobody knew he was there. He had to go on.

He walked over to the desk. The book that he had signed on his first evening at the school was still in its place and with a shaking hand he opened it. He tried to lick his thumb but his mouth was as dry as sandpaper. His eye fell at once on the last three names: DAVID ELIOT, JILL GREEN, JEFFREY JOSEPH. Although they had faded from red to brown, they were still fresher than the names on the other pages. Leaning over the desk, he began to read.

It took him about thirty seconds to realize that there wasn't one single name in the book that he recognized. There was no William Rufus, no Bessie Duncan or Roger Bacon. So he had been right. The other pupils had taken false names some time after their arrival. The only question was – why?

He closed the book. Something else had attracted his attention, lying at the far corner of the desk. It hadn't been there that first night. In fact David had never seen one before, at least not off someone's hand. It was a ring, a special ring with a black stone set in plain gold. David reached out for it ... and yelled. The ring was white-hot. It was as if it had just come out of the forge. It was impossible, of course. The ring had been lying there on the wooden surface ever since he had come into the room. It had to be some sort of illusion. But illusion or not, his fingers were still burnt, the skin blistering.

"What are you doing here?"

David twisted round, the pain momentarily forgotten. Mr Kilgraw was standing in the room – but that was impossible too. The door hadn't opened. David had heard nothing. The assistant headmaster was dressed as usual in black and white as if he was on his way to a funeral. His voice had sounded curious rather than hostile but there could be no mistaking the menace in his eyes. Clutching his hand, David desperately grappled for an excuse. *Ah well*, he thought to himself. *Refrigerator, here I come.*

"What are you doing here, David?" Mr Kilgraw asked for a second time.

"I ... I ... I was looking for you, sir."

"Why?"

"Um..." David had a flash of inspiration. "To wish you a happy Christmas, sir."

Mr Kilgraw's lips twitched in a faintly upwardly direction. "That's a very charming thought," he muttered in a tone of voice that actually said, "A likely story!" He gestured at David's hand. "You seem to have burnt yourself."

"Yes, sir." David blushed guiltily. "I saw the ring and..."

Mr Kilgraw moved forward into the room. David was careful to avoid glancing in the mirror. He knew what he would see – or rather, what he wouldn't see. He waited in silence as the assistant headmaster sat down behind the desk, wondering what would happen next.

"Sometimes it's not wise to look at things we're not meant to, David," Mr Kilgraw said. "Especially when they're things that we don't understand." He reached out and picked up the ring. David winced, but it lay there quite coolly in the palm of his hand. "I have to say that I am very disappointed in you," Mr Kilgraw went on. "Despite the little talk we had, it seems that you aren't making any progress at all."

"Then why don't you expel me?" David asked, surprising himself with his sudden defiance. But then there was nothing he would have liked more.

"Oh no! Nobody is ever expelled from Groosham Grange." Mr Kilgraw chuckled to himself. "We have had difficult children in the past, but they come to accept us ... as you will one day."

"But what do you want with me?" David couldn't contain himself any longer. "What's going on here? I know this isn't a real school. There's something horrible going on. Why won't you let me leave? I never asked to come here. Why won't you let me go and forget I ever existed? I hate it here. I hate all of you. And I'm never going to accept you, not so long as I live."

"And how long will that be?" Suddenly Mr Kilgraw's voice was ice. Each syllable had come out as a deadly whisper. David froze, feeling the tears welling up behind his eyes. But he was certain about one thing. He wouldn't cry. Not while he was in front of Mr Kilgraw.

But then it was as if Mr Kilgraw relented. He threw down the ring and sat back in his chair. When he spoke again, his voice was softer.

"There is so much that you don't understand, David," he said. "But one day things will be different. Right now you'd better get that hand looked at by Mrs Windergast."

He raised a skeletal finger to the side of his mouth, thinking for a moment in silence. "Tell her that I suggest her special ointment," he went on. "I'm sure you'll find it will give you a most ... refreshing night's sleep."

David turned round and left the study.

It was quite late by now and as usual there was nobody around in the corridors. David made his way upstairs, deep in thought. One thing was sure. He had no intention of visiting

Mrs Windergast. If Mr Kilgraw was keeping fresh blood in his refrigerator, who knows what he might find in her medicine cupboard? His hand was hurting him badly. But any pain was preferable to another session with the staff of Groosham Grange.

He was therefore annoyed to find the matron waiting for him outside her surgery. There must have been some sort of internal telephone system in the school because she already knew what had happened to him.

"Let me have a look at your poor little hand," she trilled. "Come inside and sit down while I get a plaster. We don't want it going septic, do we? My husband went septic – God rest his soul. All of him! It was a horrible sight at the end, I can tell you. And it only began with the teeniest scratch..." She ushered David into the surgery even as she spoke, giving him no chance to argue. "Now you sit down," she commanded, "while I open my medicine box."

David sat down. The surgery was small and cosy with a gas fire, a colourful rug and home-made cushions on the chairs. Embroideries hung on the wall and there were comics scattered on a low coffee table. David took all this in while the matron busied herself at the far end, rummaging in a mirror-fronted cabinet.

As she opened it, David caught the reflection of a bird on a perch. For a moment he thought he had imagined it, but then he turned round and saw the real thing, next to the window. The bird was a black crow. At first David assumed it to be stuffed, like the animals in the library. But then it croaked and shook its wings. David shivered, remembering the crow he had seen in his garden the day he had left home.

"That's Wilfred," Mrs Windergast explained as she sat down next to him. "Some people have goldfish. Some people have hamsters. But I've always preferred crows. My husband never liked him very much. In fact it was Wilfred who scratched him. Sometimes he can be very naughty! Now – let's have a look at that hand."

David held out his burnt hand and for the next few minutes Mrs Windergast busied herself with antiseptic creams and plasters. "There!" she exclaimed when she had finished. "That's better!"

David made to stand up, but the matron motioned at him to stay where he was.

"And tell me, my dear," she said. "How are you finding Groosham Grange?"

David was tired. He was fed up playing games. So he told her the truth. "All the kids are weird," he said. "The staff are crazy. The island is horrible. And the school is like something out of a horror film and I wish I was back at home."

Mrs Windergast beamed at him. "But otherwise you're perfectly happy?" she asked.

"Mrs Windergast—"

The matron held up her hand, stopping him. "Of course I understand, my dear," she said. "It's always difficult at first. That's why I've decided to let you have a bit of my special ointment."

"What does it do?" David asked suspiciously.

"It just helps you get a good night's sleep." She had produced a tub of ointment out of her apron pocket, and before David could stop her she unscrewed the lid and held it out to him. The ointment was thick and charcoal grey but surprisingly it smelt rather pleasant. It was a bitter smell, some sort of wild herb. But even the scent of it somehow relaxed him and made him feel warm inside. "Just rub it into your forehead," Mrs Windergast coaxed him, and now her voice was soft and far away. "It'll do wonders for you, just you wait and see."

David did as he was told. He couldn't refuse. He didn't *want* to refuse. The ointment felt warm against his skin. And the moment it was on, it seemed to sink through, spreading into the flesh and all the way through to his bones.

"Now you just pop into bed, David." Was it still Mrs Windergast talking? He could have sworn it was a different voice. "And have lots of lovely dreams."

David did dream that night.

He remembered undressing and getting into bed and then he must have been asleep except that his eyes were open and he was aware of things happening around him. The other boys in his dormitory were getting out of bed. Of course, that was no surprise. David rolled over and closed his eyes.

At least, that was what he meant to do. But the next thing he remembered, he was fully dressed and following them, walking downstairs towards the library. He stumbled at the top of the stairs and felt a hand steady him. It was William Rufus. David smiled. The other boy smiled back.

And then they were in the library. What happened next was confusing. He was looking at himself in a mirror – the mirror that hung opposite the fireplace. But then he walked into the mirror, right into the glass. He expected it to break. But it didn't break. And then he was on the other side. He looked behind him. William Rufus tugged at his arm. He went on.

Walls of solid rock. A twisting path going

deeper and deeper into the ground. The smell of salt water in the air. The dream had become fragmented now. It was as if the mirror had broken after all and he was seeing only the reflections in the shattered pieces. Now he was in some huge chamber, far underground. He could see the stalagmites, a glistening silver, soaring out of the ground, reaching up to the stalactites that hung down from above. Or was it the other way round...?

A great bonfire burnt in the cave, throwing fantastic shadows against the wall. The whole school had congregated there, waiting in silence for something ... or someone. Then a man stepped out from behind a slab of natural stone. And that was one thing David could not bring himself to look at, for it was more horrible than anything he had yet seen at Groosham Grange. But later on he would remember...

Two headmasters, but only one desk, only one chair.

The dream disconnected in the way that dreams do. Words were spoken. Then there was a banquet, a Christmas dinner like no other he had ever had before. Meat sizzled on the open fire. Wine flowed from silver jugs. There were puddings and pastries and pies and for the first time the pupils at Groosham Grange laughed and shouted and acted like they were actually alive. Music welled out of the ground and David looked for Jill. To his surprise he found her and they danced together for what seemed like hours, although he knew (because it was a dream) that it might have been only minutes.

And then finally there was a hush and everybody stood still as a single figure pressed through the crowds towards the stone slab. David wanted to call out but he had no voice. It was Jeffrey. Mr Kilgraw was waiting for him and he had the ring. Jeffrey was smiling, happier than David had ever seen him. He took the ring and put it on. And then, as one, the whole school began to cheer, the voices echoing against the walls, and it was with the clamour in his ears that...

David woke up.

He had a headache and there was an unpleasant taste in his mouth. He rubbed his eyes, wondering where he was. It was morning. The cold winter sun was streaming in through the windows. Slowly, he propped himself up in bed and looked around.

And he was in bed, in his usual place in the dormitory. His clothes were just as he had left them the night before. He looked at his hand. The plaster was still neatly in place. All around him, the other boys were dressing, their faces as blank as ever. David threw back the covers. It really had been no more than a dream. He half-smiled to himself. Walking through mirrors? Dancing with Jill in some underground cavern? Of course it had been a dream. How could it have been anything else?

He got out of bed and stretched. He was unusually stiff this morning, as if he had just completed a twenty mile run. He glanced to one side. Jeffrey was sitting on the bed next to him, already half-dressed. David thought back to their parting in the library and sighed. He had some making up to do.

"Good morning, Jeffrey," he said.

"Good morning, David." Jeffrey sounded almost hostile.

"Look – I just wanted to say I'm sorry about yesterday. All right?"

"There's no need to apologize, David." Jeffrey pulled his shirt on. "Just forget it."

In that brief moment David noticed a lot of things. But they all rushed in on him so quickly that he would never be quite sure which came first.

Jeffrey had changed.

He didn't just sound hostile. He was hostile. His voice had become as bleak and distant as all the others.

He wasn't stuttering any more.

And the hand that was buttoning up his shirt was different too.

It was wearing a black ring.

A LETTER

On Boxing Day, David sat down and wrote a letter to his father.

Groosham Grange,
Skrull Island,
Norfolk

26th December

Dear Father,

This is a very difficult letter to write.

It was so difficult, in fact, that he tore up the first sentence three times before he was satisfied and even then he wasn't sure that he had spelled "difficult" correctly.

I know that I have always been a disappointment

to you. I have never been interested in merchant banking and I was expelled from Beton College. But I now see that I was wrong.

I have decided to get a job as a teller in the Bank of England. If the Bank of England won't have me I'll try the Bank of Germany. I'm sure you'd be proud of me if I were A Teller the Hun.

He crossed out the last sentence too. Then the bell for lunch went and it was another hour before he could sit down and begin the next paragraph.

But there is something I have to ask you.

PLEASE TAKE ME AWAY FROM GROOSHAM GRANGE. It's not that I don't like it here (although I don't like it at all). But it's not at all what you were expecting. If you knew what it was really like here, you'd never have sent me in the first place.

I think they are involved in black magic. Mr Kilgraw, the assistant headmaster, is a vampire. Mr Creer, who teaches pottery, religious studies and maths, is dead, and Miss Pedicure, who teaches English and history, ought to be, as she is at least six hundred years old! You'll think I'm mad when you read this ...

David read it back and decided that he quite possibly was. Could all this really be happening to him?

101

... but I promise you, I'm telling the truth. I think they want to turn me into some sort of zombie like they did to my friend Jeffrey. He won't talk to me any more. He won't even stutter to me. And I know that if I stay here much longer, I'll be next.

David took a deep breath. His hand was aching and he realized that he was clutching the pen so hard that it was a miracle the ink was reaching the nib. Forcing himself to relax, he pulled the page towards him and began again.

I can't describe all the things that have happened to me since I got here. But I've been stabbed, drugged, threatened and half-scared to death. I know Grandpa used to do all this to you when you were young, but I don't think it's fair when I haven't done anything wrong and I don't want to be a zombie. Please at least visit the school. Then you'll see what I mean.

I can't post this letter to you because there's no postbox on the island and if you've written to me, I haven't got it. I'm going to give this to a friend of mine, Jill Green.

She's planning to escape tomorrow and has promised to send it to you. I've also given her your telephone number and she'll call you (reversing the charges). She'll be able to tell you everything that's happened and I just hope you believe her.

I must stop now as it's time for the afternoon lesson - chemistry. We're being taught the secret of life.

Help!

Your son,
David

At least nobody had come into the library while he was writing. David had been scribbling the words with one eye on the door and the other on the mirror with the result that the lines had gone all over the place and reading them again made him feel seasick. But it would have to do. He folded the page in half and then in half again. He didn't have an envelope but Jill had promised to buy one – along with a stamp – as soon as she reached the mainland.

If all went according to plan, Captain Bloodbath would arrive at ten o'clock the following morning. Jill would skip the second lesson and hide near the jetty. As soon as Gregor had unloaded the supplies and driven the captain up to the school, she would slip on to the boat and underneath the rags. The boat would leave at eleven. And by midday Jill would be well on her way, hitchhiking south. She had to get away. She was his only hope. But that wasn't the only worry in David's mind as he hurried along to the chemistry laboratory. She might send the letter. His father might read it. But would he believe it? Would anyone believe it?

David still wasn't sure if he believed it himself.

THE INSPECTOR

Jill didn't even get off the island.

She was discovered by Captain Bloodbath huddling under the rags and was jerked, trembling and miserable, back on to dry land.

"So you thought you could fool me, my pretty?" he exclaimed with a leering grin. "Thought I didn't know the waterline of my own boat? I'd know if there was an extra sprat on board. Hitch a free ride to the mainland – is that what you had in mind? Well, you'd have to sail a few high seas before you could bamboozle a Bloodbath!"

For a whole week after that, Jill waited in trepidation for something to happen to her. As David had somewhat unhelpfully told her, if you were caught trying to run away from Beton College, your head was shaved and you had to spend a month walking round with your shoelaces tied together. But in fact nothing happened. There really were no punishments at Groosham Grange. If Captain Bloodbath had even bothered to mention the incident to any of the staff, they didn't take the slightest bit of notice.

And so the two of them were still there as the snow melted and the winter dripped and trickled its way towards spring. They had been on the island now for seven weeks. Nothing about the school had changed – they were still both out-siders. But David knew that he had changed. And that frightened him.

He was beginning to enjoy his life on the island. Almost despite himself he was doing well in class. French, history, maths ... even Latin came easily to him now. He had got a place in the first eleven football team and although no other school came to the island he still enjoyed the games – even with the pig-bladder balls. And then there was Jill. David depended on her as much as she did on him. They spent all their free time together, walking and talking. And she had become the closest friend he had ever had.

So he was almost grateful that her escape had failed – and it was that that worried him. Despite the sunshine and the first scent of spring, something evil was going on at Groosham Grange. And slowly, surely, it was drawing him in. If he liked it there now, how long would it be before he became a part of it too?

Jill kept him sane. Operation Bottle was her idea. Every day for a week they stole whatever bottles they could get their hands on and then threw them into the sea with messages asking for help. They sent bottles to their parents, to the police, to the Department of Education and even, in one desperate moment, to the Queen. David was fairly certain that the bottles would sink long before they reached the coast of Norfolk or at least get washed back up on the island. But he was wrong. One of the bottles arrived.

It was Mr Leloup who announced the news.

The French teacher was a small, bald, timid-looking man. At least, he was small, bald and timid-looking at the start of the month. But as the full moon approached, he would gradually change. His body would swell out like the Incredible Hulk, his face would become increasingly ferocious and he would develop a full head of hair. Then, when the full moon came, he would disappear altogether, only to appear the next day back to square one. All his clothes had been torn and stitched together so many times that he must have been surrounded by at least a mile of thread. When he got angry in class – and he did have a very short temper – he didn't shout. He barked.

He was angry that morning, the first day in February.

"It would appear zat the school 'as a leetle prob-lame," he announced in his exaggerated French accent. "The busybodies een the Department of Education 'av decide-dead to pay us a viseet. So tomorrow we must albee on our best be-evure." He glanced meaningfully at Jill and David. "And no-buddy is to speak to zis man unless 'ee speaks to them."

That evening, Jill was hardly able to contain her excitement.

"He must have got one of our messages," Jill said. "If the Department of Education find out the truth about Groosham Grange, they'll close it down and that will be the end of it. We'll be free!"

"I know," David muttered gloomily. "But they won't let us anywhere near him. And if they see us talking to him, they'll probably do something terrible to him. And to us."

Jill looked at him scornfully. "Have you lost your bottle?" she demanded.

"Of course I haven't," David said. "How else do you think he got the message?"

Mr Netherby arrived on the island the next

morning. A thin, neat man in a grey suit with spectacles and a leather briefcase, he was ferried over by Captain Bloodbath and met by Mr Kilgraw. He gave them a small, official smile and a brief, official handshake and then began his official visit. He was very much the official. Wherever he went he took notes, occasionally asking questions and jotting down the answers in a neat, official hand.

To David and Jill's disgust, the whole school had put on a show for him. It was like a royal visit to a hospital when the floors are all scrubbed and the really sick patients are taken off their life support machines and hidden away in cupboards. Everything that Mr Netherby saw was designed to impress. The staff were all in their best suits and the pupils seemed lively, interested and – above all – normal. He was formally introduced to a few of them and they answered his questions with just the right amount of enthusiasm. Yes, they were very happy at Groosham Grange. Yes, they were working hard. No, they had never thought of running away.

Mr Netherby was delighted by what he saw. He couldn't fail to be. As the day wore on he gradually unwound and even the sight of Gregor, humping a sack of potatoes down to the kitchen, only delighted him all the more.

"The Council is very keen on the employment of disabled people," he was heard to remark. "He wouldn't by any chance be gay as well?"

"He's certainly very queer," Mr Kilgraw concurred.

"Excellent! Excellent! First class!" Mr Netherby nodded and ticked off a page in his notebook.

By the end of the day, the inspector was in a thoroughly good mood. Although he had been sorry not to meet the heads – Mr Kilgraw had told him that they were away at a conference – he seemed entirely satisfied by everything he had seen. David and Jill watched him in dismay. Their only chance seemed to be slipping away and there was nothing they could do about it. Mr Kilgraw had managed things so that they had never been allowed near him. He hadn't visited any of their classes. And whenever they had drawn near him, he had been quickly steered in the opposite direction.

"It's now or never," Jill whispered as Mr Kilgraw led his visitor towards the front door. They had just finished prep and had half an hour's free time before bed. Jill was clutching a note. She and David had written it the evening before and then carefully folded it into a square. The note read: THINGS ARE NOT WHAT THEY SEEM AT GROOSHAM GRANGE. YOU ARE IN

GREAT DANGER. MEET US ON THE CLIFFS AT 7.45 P.M. DO NOT LET ANYONE ELSE SEE THIS NOTE.

Mr Kilgraw and the inspector were walking down the corridor towards them.

"A most enjoyable day," Mr Netherby was saying. "However, I have to tell you, Mr Kilgraw, that my department is rather concerned that we have no record of Groosham Grange. You don't even appear to have a licence."

"Is that a problem?" Mr Kilgraw asked.

"I fear so. There'll have to be an enquiry. But I can assure you that I'll be filing a most favourable report..."

Jill and David knew what they had to do.

They moved at the same time, walking swiftly into the corridors as if they were hurrying to get somewhere. Halfway down they bumped into the two men who had stood aside to let them pass. At that moment, David pretended to lose his balance, knocking Mr Kilgraw back into the lockers. At the same time, Jill pressed the square of paper into Mr Netherby's hand.

"Sorry, sir," David muttered.

It had taken less than three seconds. Then they were moving away again as if nothing had happened. But the assistant headmaster hadn't seen anything. Mr Netherby had the note. The only question was, would he turn up at the cliffs?

As soon as the two men had turned the corner, Jill and David doubled back, then left the school through a side exit that led into the cemetery. Nobody saw them go.

"What's the time?" David asked.

"Quarter past seven."

"Then we've got half an hour..."

They ran across the playing fields, past the lake and into the forest. It was a warm, cloudless night. The moon lit their path as they raced for the cover of the trees but neither of them looked up, neither of them saw.

It was a full moon.

They stopped, panting, at the edge of the forest.

"Are you sure this is a good idea?" David asked.

"We've got to come this way," Jill said. "If we take the road, somebody may see us."

"But this forest gives me the creeps."

"The whole island gives me the creeps."

They pressed on through the forest. Here, with the moon shut out by a ceiling of leaves, everything was very dark and very still. It was like no forest David had ever seen. The trees seemed to be tied together in knots, thorns and briars snaking round the ancient trunks. Fantastic mushrooms bulged out of the ground only to ooze a horrible yellow when they trod on them. Nothing stirred: not a bird, not an owl, not a breath of wind.

Then the wolf howled.

Jill seized hold of David so suddenly that she nearly tore off his shirt. "What is it?" she whispered.

"I think it was a dog," David whispered back.

"I've never heard a dog like that."

"It sounded like a dog."

"You're sure?"

"Of course I'm sure."

The wolf howled again.

They ran.

They ran whichever way they could, dodging under the low-lying branches and leaping over the undergrowth. Soon they were hopelessly lost. The forest had swallowed them up, an impossible maze that seemed to grow even as they fought their way through it. And the animal, whatever it was, was getting closer. David couldn't see it. He almost wished he could. Instead he sensed it and that was much, much worse. His imagination screamed at him. The wolf, hooking its claws into the flesh at the back of his neck. The wolf, snarling ferociously as its drooling jaws lunged at his throat. The wolf...

"We can't go on!" Jill almost sobbed the words, sliding to a halt.

David stopped beside her, breathless, his shirt soaked with sweat. Why had they ever decided to come this way? He had stumbled and fallen into a bed of thistles and his right hand was on fire. And their twisting path had led them into a dead end of branch and bramble. David looked around him. A heavy stick lay on the ground, blown down in one of the storms. Clutching it with both hands, he dragged it free of the nettles and picked it up.

"David...!"

He turned round. And now he could see something. It was too dark to tell what it was. A wolf, a man ... or something between the two? It was just a shape, a mass of black fur with two red eyes glowing in the centre. He could hear it too. A soft, snuffling sound that made his skin crawl.

There was no way back. The creature was blocking the path.

But there was no way forward.

The creature leapt.

David swung the stick.

He had shut his eyes at the last second, but he felt the heavy piece of wood make contact. His arm shuddered. The creature screamed. Then there was a sound of the undergrowth crashing and breaking and when he opened his eyes again it had gone.

Jill stepped forward and laid a hand on his shoulder.

"That was no dog," she said.

"Then what was it?"

"I don't know." Jill looked thoughtfully back up the path. "But it howled with a French accent."

They had reached the southern end of the island where the land sloped steeply down, curving round to the point. Climbing through the last tangles of the forest, they crossed the road and ran to the end of the cliffs, where they had arranged to meet Mr Netherby. Jill glanced at her watch. They had made it with ten minutes to spare.

They waited there, high up above the sea.

The top of the cliff was flat and peaceful with a soft carpet of grass. Twenty metres below, the waves glittered in the moonlight, splashing against the rocks that jutted out, looking as if they had torn through the very fabric of the sea.

"Do you think he'll come?" David asked.

"I think he's already here," Jill said.

There was somebody walking across the grass towards them, a black silhouette against the pale sky. He was still about two hundred yards away but as he drew closer they saw that he was clutching an attaché case. Seeing them, he stopped and glanced over his shoulder. The man was afraid. They could tell simply from the way he walked.

He had covered about fifty yards, following the edge of the cliff, when it happened. At first David thought he had been stung by a wasp. But then he remembered that it was only March and there were no wasps. The man jerked, his head snapping back. One hand reached for the side of his neck. Then it happened a second time, only this time it was his shoulder. He clutched it, spinning round as if he had been shot. But there had been no gunshot. There was nobody in sight.

The man – and it was Mr Netherby – screamed as one of his knees gave way beneath him, his voice thin and high-pitched. Then it was his back. Falling to the ground he arched up and screamed again, both hands clawing at the air.

"What's wrong with him?" Jill whispered, her eyes wide and staring.

David shook his head, unable to speak.

It was a dreadful sight made more dreadful by the stillness of the night and the soft witness of the moon. Mr Netherby was jerking about like an out-of-control puppet as first one part of his body, then the next, was attacked. Jill and David could only stand and watch. When it seemed that Mr Netherby must be dead, he reached out and grabbed his attaché case, then somehow staggered to his feet. For a moment he stood there, swaying on the very edge of the cliff.

"I shall have to report this!" he called out.

Then something struck him in the heart and he toppled backwards into the darkness, plummeting down to the rocks.

David and Jill said nothing for a very long time. Then David gently put his hand round her shoulders. "We'd better go back," he said.

But for David the night was not yet over.

They had slipped into the school unnoticed and whispered a trembling "good night" in the corridor. The other boys had already gone to bed and were sleeping as David undressed and slipped between the sheets. But he couldn't fall asleep. For what seemed like hours he lay there, thinking about what had happened and wondering what would happen next. Then he heard it.

"David..."

It was his own name, whispered in the darkness by someone who was not there. He turned over and buried his head in the pillow, certain that he must have imagined it.

"David..."

There it was again, soft, insistent, not just in his ear but inside his very head. He sat upright and looked around him. Nobody stirred.

"David, come to us..."

He had to obey. Almost in a trance he got out of bed, put on his dressing-gown and crept noiselessly out of the dormitory. The school was swathed in darkness but downstairs in the main hall he could see an open doorway with a solid rectangle of light stretching out on to the carpet. That was where the voice wanted him to go ... into the staff room. He hesitated, afraid of what he would find inside, but the voice urged him on. He had to obey.

He walked down the staircase and, without knocking, entered the room. There, in the harsh light, the trance ended as David found himself face to face with the entire staff of Groosham Grange.

Mrs Windergast was sitting in an armchair closest to the door, knitting. Next to her sat Mr Creer, his eyes closed, scarcely breathing.

Gregor crouched beside the fireplace, muttering to himself. Opposite the fireplace, Mr Leloup was also seated, one side of his face purple and swollen. David remembered the creature in the wood, how he had beaten it off, and he was not surprised when the French teacher glanced at him with venom in his eyes. But it was Miss Pedicure who drew his attention. She was sitting at a table in the middle of the room and as David came in she giggled and threw something down. It was a wax model, thin, with spectacles, clutching a tiny wax attaché case. Pins had been stuck into its neck, its arms, its legs and its chest with one pin – the thirteenth – buried in its heart.

"Please come in, David."

Mr Kilgraw was standing in front of the window with his back to the room. Now he turned round and walked back into the room, pausing at the end of the table. His eyes flickered from David to the wax doll. "Did you really think that you could fool us?" he said. There was no menace in his voice. His tone was almost matter-of-fact. But the menace was still there in the room, swirling through the air like cigarette smoke. "When you wrote that letter, you signed Mr Netherby's death warrant. Regrettable, but you gave us no choice."

He raised his head and now his eyes settled on David.

"What are we going to do with you, David? You are doing well in class. You are, I think, beginning to enjoy yourself on the island. But still you resist us. We have your body. We have your mind. But you still refuse to give us your spirit."

David opened his mouth to speak but Mr Kilgraw silenced him with one gesture of his hand.

"We are running out of time," he said. "In fact

we have only a few days remaining. I would be sad to lose you, David. We all would. And that is why I have decided on desperate measures."

Mr Kilgraw picked up the doll and plucked the pin out of its heart. A single drop of bright red blood dripped onto the table.

"You will report to the study at one o'clock tomorrow," he said. "I think it's time you saw the heads."

THE HEADS

I think it's time you saw the heads.

David had overheard the heads talking. He had been inside their study. But in all his time on the island he had never once seen Mr Fitch or Mr Teagle.

He hardly got a wink of sleep that night. Somewhere in the back of his mind he was angry. It wasn't fair. The bottles had been Jill's idea, so why had he been singled out? And what would the heads do with him when they got him? At Beton College any visit to the head-master invariably meant six strokes of the cane. Even at the end-of-term sherry party he would generally cane several of the boys and even, on one memorable occasion, a couple of the parents. And there were two headmasters at Groosham Grange. Did that mean he could expect twelve?

He finally fell asleep at about two o'clock.

It was a troubled sleep with dreams of wolves and black rings and mirrors with no reflections. At one point in the dream he was standing on the cliffs watching Mr Netherby fall. Only it was he who was holding the wax doll, he who was jabbing the pins into it. Then his father wheelchaired himself across the grass, waving a packet of muesli, and David pointed at him and muttered something he didn't understand and his father exploded in flames and...

He woke up.

The day dragged on like a sack of bricks. Maths, then history, then English literature... David didn't see Jill all morning which, in his present mood, was probably just as well. He hardly took in a word that was said to him. He could only think of his appointment and his eyes were drawn to the clocks on the classroom walls. The minute hands seemed to be moving slower than they should have been. And the other pupils knew. Every now and then he caught them glancing at him. Then they would whisper among themselves. The teachers did their best to ignore him.

At last the time came. David was tempted to run away and hide – but he knew it would do him no good. The staff would find him and drag him out and whatever they might think of him, he didn't want to act like a coward. At one o'clock exactly he stood outside the headmasters' study. He took a deep breath. He raised his hand. He knocked. "Come ..."

"... in."

Both of them had spoken, Mr Fitch taking the first word, Mr Teagle the second. David went in.

The sun must have passed behind a cloud for it was dark in the room, the light barely penetrating the stained glass windows. The black marble floor, too, made the study seem darker than it had any right to be in the middle of the day. David closed the door behind him and moved slowly towards the desk. There were two men sitting behind it, waiting for him.

No. One man.

But...

And then David saw with a spidery surge of horror that brushed against the bottom of his spine and scuttled all the way up to his neck. There was only one headmaster at Groosham Grange – but two heads. Or to put it another way, the heads really were heads. Mr Fitch was quite bald with a hooked nose and vulture eyes. Mr Teagle had thin grey hair, a tiny beard and glasses. But the two heads were joined to one body, sitting in a dark suit and bright green tie behind the single desk in the single chair. The two heads had a neck in the shape of a letter Y.

Even as David fainted he found himself wondering which of them had chosen the tie.

He woke up back in the dormitory, lying on his own bed.

"Are you feeling better, my dear?"

Mrs Windergast was sitting on the bed next to him, holding a sponge and a basin and watching him anxiously. She had loosened his collar and mopped his face with cold water.

"You obviously weren't quite ready to see the heads," the matron crooned on. "It can be a very upsetting experience. Poor Mr Fitch and Mr Teagle were both so distinguished and good-looking until their little accident."

If that was a "little" accident, David thought to himself, what would you call a major calamity?

"We're all very worried about you, David." Mrs Windergast leaned forward with the sponge but David reared away. It might only be water in the basin, but at Groosham Grange you never knew. One quick slosh and you might wake up with three extra eyes and a passion for fresh blood.

The matron sighed and dropped the sponge.

"The trouble is," she said, "we've got to you rather late, and now we don't have much time left. How long now? Two days only! It would be such a shame to lose you, really it would. I think you're a nice boy, David. I really wish...!"

"Just leave me alone!" David turned his eyes away from her. He couldn't bear looking at her. Mrs Windergast might be just like somebody's grandmother. But the somebody was probably Jack the Ripper.

"All right, dear. I can see you're still upset..."

Mrs Windergast stood up and bustled out of the dormitory.

David stayed where he was, glad to be alone. He needed time to think, time to work things out. Already the memory of the headmasters had faded, as if his brain were unwilling to hold on to the image. Instead he thought about what Mrs Windergast had just told him. "Two days only." Why only two days?

And then it clicked. He should have realized at once. Today was March 2. Without any holidays and with no post arriving on the island, it was all too easy to forget the date. But March 4 – in two days' time – was one day he could never forget. It was his birthday, his thirteenth birthday.

And then he remembered something else. Once, when he was chatting to Jeffrey – that was when he was still able to chat to Jeffrey – the fat boy had mentioned that he was unlucky enough to have a birthday that fell on Christmas Day. In the rush of events he had managed to forget all about it, but now he remembered. It had been on Christmas Day that Jeffrey had changed. That was when he had been given his black ring. On his thirteenth birthday.

In just two days' time, David's own turn would come. Either he would accept the ring and all that came with it or...

But he couldn't even consider the alternative.

David swung himself off the bed and got to his feet. He couldn't wait any longer. He had no more time. He knew he had to escape from Groosham Grange. He knew when he had to go.

And suddenly he knew how.

ESCAPE!

The next day, one day before David's thirteenth birthday, Captain Bloodbath returned to the island. It was a Tuesday and he had brought with him three crates of supplies. There was to be a big party the following night – and David had no doubt that he was supposed to be the guest of honour. But he had no intention of being there. If things worked out the way he hoped, the guest of honour would be on a train to London before anyone guessed!

The sun was already setting as he and Jill crouched behind a sand dune, watching Gregor and the captain unload the last of the crates. The boat had arrived late that day. But it was there – David's last chance. He had hardly uttered a word since his encounter with the heads, and Jill, too, had been strangely silent as if she was upset about something. But it was she

126

who finally broke the silence.

"It's not going to work," she said. "I told you, David. There's nowhere you can hide on the boat. Not without him noticing."

"We're not going to hide on the boat," David replied.

"Well, what *are* we going to do then? Steal it?"

"Exactly."

Jill stared at him, wondering if he was joking. But David's face was pale and serious.

"Steal the boat?" she whispered.

"When we first came to the island, he left his keys in the ignition. I noticed then." David ran a dry tongue over dry lips. "It's the last thing anybody would expect. And it's our only hope."

"But do you know how to steer a boat?"

"No. But it can't be very different from a car."

"You can't drown in a car!"

David took one last quick glance back up the cliffs. Gregor and the captain had disappeared and there was no sound of the Jeep. He tapped Jill on the shoulder and they ran forward together, the shingle crunching under their feet. The boat was bobbing up and down beside the jetty. Captain Bloodbath hadn't dropped anchor but he had tied the boat to a bollard with a knot that looked like six snakes in a washing machine.

Ignoring it for the moment, David climbed on board and went over to the steering wheel, searching for the keys. The deck swayed underneath him and for a horrible moment he thought that he'd been wrong from the start – that the captain had taken the keys with him. But then the boat swayed the other way and he saw the key-ring, an emerald skull, swaying at the end of a chain. The key was jutting out of the ignition. He let out a deep breath. In just a few minutes they would be away.

"How does it work?"

Jill had got on to the boat and was standing beside him, her voice challenging him to explain. David ran his eyes over the controls. There was a steering wheel – that was easy enough – and a lever that presumably sent the boat either backwards or forwards. But as for the rest of the buttons and switches, the dials and the compass, they could have been designed to send the boat on a one-way journey to the moon and David wouldn't have been any the wiser.

"So how does it work?" Jill asked again.

"It isn't difficult." David glanced at her irritably. "You just turn the key..."

"Then why don't you?"

"I'm going to."

He did.

Nothing happened.

David turned it again, twisting it so hard that he almost bent it in half. But still the engine refused to cough or even whimper.

"We could always swim..." Jill began.

At the same moment, David reached out and hit a large red button above the key. At once the engine chugged noisily to life, the water bubbling and smoking at the stern.

"I'll see to the knot..." David began, moving away from the wheel.

"No." Jill leant down and snatched up a fish gutting knife that had been lying on the deck. "You stay with the controls. I'll see to the knot."

The boat was tied at the very front and to reach the rope Jill had to climb back over the edge and on to the jetty. She stopped beside the bollard and set to work. It was a sharp knife but it was also a thick rope and although she sawed back and forth with all her strength she didn't seem to be getting anywhere. David waited for her on the boat, the wooden planks of the deck humming and vibrating beneath him. The engine seemed to be noisier than ever. Would they hear it back at the school? He looked up.

And froze.

Captain Bloodbath was coming back. The sound of the engine must have been carried up and over the cliff by the wind. Or perhaps he and Jill had been missed from tea? Either way, the result was the same. They had been discovered and Captain Bloodbath and Gregor were speeding down the road in the Jeep, heading in their direction.

"Jill!" David called out.

But she had seen them already. "Stay where you are!" she shouted back and doubled her efforts, sawing at the rope like a berserk violinist. By now she had cut halfway through, but Gregor and the captain were getting closer with every second that passed. Already they were approaching the bottom of the cliffs. It would take them only another twenty seconds to reach the jetty.

Jill glanced up, took a quick breath, then bent over the rope again, hacking, stabbing and slicing with the knife. The rope was fraying now, the strands separating. But still it refused to part completely.

"Hurry!" David shouted.

There was nothing he could do. His legs had turned to stone. The jeep reached the end of the jetty and screeched to a halt. Captain Bloodbath and Gregor leapt out. Jill's face twisted with fear, her hair blowing in the wind. But she still sawed. The knife bit into the rope. Another strand broke free.

Gregor was slightly ahead of the captain, his

feet clambering down the jetty towards her. Jill cried out and sliced down the knife.

The rope broke in half.

"Jill!" David called out.

But it was too late. Gregor had leapt forward like a human toad and now he was on her. Before Jill could move, his arms and legs were around her, dragging her to the ground.

"Go, David! Go!" she screamed.

David's hand slammed down on the lever. He felt the boat lurch underneath him as the propeller boiled the water. The boat slid out backwards into the open sea, trailing the broken rope across the jetty.

Then Captain Bloodbath dived forward. With a yell of triumph his hands found the rope and clamped shut on it.

The boat was several feet out now. Jill was watching it with despairing eyes, pinned down on the jetty by the dwarf. Gregor was cackling horribly, his single eye bulging. The engine screamed. The propeller churned up white water and mud. But the boat was going nowhere. Captain Bloodbath was holding on to it, digging his heels into the wood, like a cowboy with a wild stallion. His mouth was set in a grimace. His face had gone crimson. David couldn't believe what he was seeing. The captain had to let go! He couldn't possibly stand the strain – not with the engine at full strength.

But he hadn't pushed the reverse lever all the way down. An inch remained. With a cry of despair, David threw himself on to it, forcing it the rest of the way.

Captain Bloodbath still held on! It was an impossible tug-of-war, a man against a boat. The boat was rearing away, almost out of the water. But the man refused to let go, his hands fixed like vices on the rope…

"Aaaaaaargh!"

Captain Bloodbath screamed. At the same moment the boat shot backwards as if catapulted.

David stared in disbelief.

The captain's hands were still clutching the rope, but they were no longer attached to his arms. The force of the engine had pulled them clean off and as the boat rocketed away they fell off, dropping into the sea with a faint splash like two pale crabs.

David twisted the wheel, feeling sick. The boat spun round. He jammed the lever forward. The water erupted. And then he was away, leaving Groosham Grange, Skrull Island, Jill and a now handless Captain Bloodbath far behind him.

THE GHOST TRAIN

David ran through the field, the grass reaching up to his armpits. Behind him the boat stood, not moored to the jetty, but buried in it. The crossing had been far from smooth.

And now it was the morning of the next day. What with the mist, the currents and the unfamiliar controls, it had taken David longer than he had thought to make the crossing and it had been dark when he had crashed into the coast of Norfolk. He had been forced to spend the night in the wrecked cabin and it was only when daylight had come that he had realized he had ended up exactly where he had begun weeks ago.

The field climbed gently upwards towards the brilliant white windmill that David had first noticed from the hearse. On closer sight, the windmill turned out to be broken-down and deserted, battered by the wind and the rain. The sails themselves were no more than frameworks of twisted wood, like skeleton insect wings. If David had been hoping to find a telephone there, he was disappointed. The windmill had died a hundred years ago and the telephone lines had passed it by.

But on the other side he found a main road and stood there swaying, cold and exhausted. A car sped past and he blinked. It was almost as if he had forgotten what an ordinary car looked like. He glanced nervously over his shoulder. There was no way that anybody could follow him from the school. But with Groosham Grange you never knew, and he felt lost and vulnerable out in the great silence of the plain.

He had to get to the nearest town and civilization. He had no money. That meant hitchhiking. David stretched out a hand and flicked up a thumb. Surely someone would stop. Someone had to stop.

Seventy-seven cars went by. David counted them all. Not only did they refuse to stop but some of them actually accelerated as if anxious to avoid him. What was wrong with him? He was just an ordinary, crumpled, tired thirteen-year-old out in the middle of nowhere trying to get a lift! Thirteen! "Happy birthday!" he muttered to himself. Grimly, he stuck his thumb out and tried again.

The seventy-eighth car stopped. It was a bright red Ford Cortina driven by a jolly, fat man called Horace Tobago. Mr Tobago, it turned out, was a travelling salesman. As he explained, he sold practical jokes and magic tricks. Not that he needed to explain. As David sat down, his seat let out a rude noise. The sweet he was offered was made of soap. And there were two doves, a rabbit and a string of rubber sausages in the glove compartment.

"So where have you come from?" Horace asked, lifting his chin to allow his bow tie to revolve.

"From school," David muttered.

"Running away?" Horace lifted his eyebrows one at a time and wiggled his nose.

"Yes." David took a deep breath. "I have to get to a police station."

"Why?"

"I'm in danger, Mr Tobago. The school is mad. It's on an island – and they're all vampires and witches and ghosts ... and they want to turn me into one of them. I've got to stop them!"

"Ha ha ha haaargh!" Horace Tobago had a laugh like a cow being strangled. His face went bright red and the flower in his buttonhole squirted water over the dashboard. "So you're a bit of a practical joker yourself, are you, David?" he exclaimed at last. "Like a bit of a giggle? Maybe I can sell you a stink bomb or a piece of plastic sick..."

"I'm telling the truth!" David protested.

"Course you are! Course you are! And my name is Count Dracula!" The joke salesman laughed again. "Vampires and witches. What a wheeze, old boy! What a wheeze!"

David got out of the car at the first town, Hunstanton. Mr Tobago had laughed so much during the journey that there were tears streaming down his cheeks and a fake wart had fallen off his chin. He was still shrieking with laughter as he drove away waving, playing-cards tumbling out of his sleeves. David waited until the car had gone. Then he set off.

Hunstanton was a resort town. In the summer it might have been full of colour and life but out of season it was something of a last resort, a tired jumble of grey slate roofs and towers, shops and pavilions sloping down a hillside to the edge of a cold and choppy sea. There was a quay with a cluster of fishing boats half-wrapped in their own nets and looking for all the world like the fish they were meant to catch. In the distance a number of grey tents and wooden boards surrounded what might, in the summer, be a fun fair. In these sunless days of spring, there was precious little fun to be seen anywhere.

He had to find a police station. But even as he began to search for one, he was struck by a nasty thought. Horace Tobago hadn't believed a word he had said. Why should the police? If he went in there spouting on about black magic and witchcraft, they would probably call the local asylum. Worse still, they might hold him there and call the school. He was thirteen years old now. And it was a fact of life that adults never believed thirteen-year-olds.

He paused and looked around him. He was standing outside a library and on an impulse he turned and went in. At least there was something he could do – find out more. The more he knew, the more he could argue his case. And books seemed the best place to start.

Unfortunately, Hunstanton Library did not have a large section on Witchcraft. In fact there were only three books on the shelf and two of them had accidentally strayed out of Handicrafts, which were on the shelf next door. But the third looked promising. It was called *Black Magic in Britain* by one Winny H. Zoothroat. David flicked through it, then carried it over to the table to read in more detail.

COVENS A gathering of witches, usually numbering thirteen or a multiple of thirteen. The main reason for this is that twelve is often considered a perfect number – so the figure thirteen comes to mean death. Thirteen is also the age at which a novice will be introduced.

INITIATION A new witch is often required to sign his or her name in a black book which is kept by the master of the coven. It is customary for the name to be signed in the novice's own blood. Once the novice has signed, he or she will be given a new name. This is the name of power and might be taken from a past witch as a mark of respect.

WITCHES Well-known witches in Britain include Roger Bacon, who was famed for walking between two Oxford spires; Bessie Dunlop, who was burned to death in Ayrshire and William Rufus, a 13th-century Master-Devil.

SABBAT The witches' sabbath – it takes place at midnight. Before setting out for the sabbat, the witches rub an ointment of hemlock and aconite into their skin. This ointment causes a dream-like state and, they believe, helps with the release of magical powers.

MAGIC The best-known magic used by witches is called "the law of similarity". In this, a wax model stands in for the victim of the witch's anger. Whatever is done to the model, the human victim will feel.

The witch's most powerful magical tool is the familiar, a creature who acts as a sort of demonic servant. The cat is the most common sort of familiar but other animals have been used, such as pigs and even crows.

David lost track of time as he sat there reading the book. But by late afternoon, he had learnt just about everything he wanted to know about Groosham Grange, as well as quite a bit that he didn't. The book had one last surprise. David was about to pick it up and return it to the shelf when it fell open on another page and his eyes alighted on an entry that leapt off the page.

GROOSHAM GRANGE *See publisher's note.*

Curiously, David turned to the end of the book. There was a brief note on the last page, written by the publisher.

When she was writing this book, Winny H. Zoothroat set out for the county of

Norfolk to research Groosham Grange, the legendary "Academy of Witchcraft", where young novices were once taught the art of Black Magic.

Unfortunately, Miss Zoothroat failed to return from her journey. Her typewriter was washed ashore a few months later. Out of respect to her memory, the publishers have decided to leave this section blank.

An academy of witchcraft! The words were still buzzing in David's head as he left the library. But what else could Groosham Grange have been? Fluent Latin, wax model-making, weird cookery and very un-Christian religious studies ... it all added up. But David had never wanted to be a witch. So why had they chosen him?

He was walking down the High Street now, past the shops which were preparing to close for the day. A movement somewhere in the corner of his eye made him stop and glance back the way he had come. For a moment he thought he had imagined it. Then the same misshapen, limping figure darted out from behind a parked car.

Gregor.

Somehow the dwarf had reached Hunstanton and David knew at once that he must be looking for him. Without even thinking, he broke into a run, down the hill and out towards the sea. If he was found, he knew what would happen to him. The school would kill him rather than let him tell his story. They had already killed twice for sure. How many other people had ended up in the cemetery at Skrull Island earlier than they had expected?

It was only when he had reached the sea front that he stopped to take a breath and forced himself to calm down. It was a coincidence. It had to be. Nobody at the school could possibly know that he was still in Hunstanton.

A few feet away from him, Gregor giggled. The hunchback was sitting on a low brick wall, watching him with one beady eye. He pulled something out of his belt. It was a knife, at least seven inches long, glinting wickedly. Still giggling, he licked the blade. David turned and ran again.

He had no idea where he was going. The whole world was swaying and shuddering each time his foot thudded against the cold concrete pavement. All he could hear was his own tortured breathing. When he looked back again, the dwarf was gone. Hunstanton lay in the distance behind him. He had reached the end of the promenade.

Sagging tents and warped wooden kiosks surrounded him. The funfair! He had wandered right into the middle of it.

"Fancy a ride, sonny?"

The speaker was an old man in a shabby coat, a cigarette dangling out of the corner of his mouth. He was standing beside the ghost train. Three carriages – blue, green and yellow – stood on the curving track in front of the swing doors.

"A ride?" David glanced from the ghost train to the sea front. There was no sign of Gregor.

"A test run." The old man squeezed his cigarette and coughed. "Bit of luck you turning up. You can have a free ride."

"No thanks..." Even as David uttered the words, Gregor appeared again, shuffling into the fairground area. He hadn't seen David yet, but he was searching. The knife was still in his hand, held low, slanting upwards.

David leapt into the carriage. He had to get out of sight. A couple of minutes on a ghost train might be enough. At least Gregor couldn't follow him in there.

"Hang on tight." The old man pressed a switch.

The carriage jerked forward.

A second later it hit the doors. They broke open, then swung shut behind it. David found himself swallowed up by the darkness. He felt as if he were suffocating. Then a light glowed red behind a plastic skull and he breathed again. If the skull was meant to frighten him, it had

had the opposite effect. It reminded him that this was just an entertainment, a cheap funfair ride with plastic masks and coloured light bulbs. A loudspeaker crackled into life with a tape-recorded "Awooo!" and David even managed a smile. A green light flicked on. A rubber spider bounced up and down on an all-too-visible wire. David smiled again.

Then the carriage plunged into a chasm.

It fell through the darkness for so long that the air rushed through David's hair and he was forced back into the seat. At the last moment, when he was sure he would be dashed to pieces at the bottom of the track, it slowed down as if hitting a cushion of air.

"Some ride..." he whispered to himself. It was a relief to hear the sound of his own voice.

Another light flashed on – a light that was somehow less electric than the ones that had gone before. A soft bubbling sound was coming out of the loudspeakers, only suddenly David wondered if there were any loudspeakers. It sounded too real. He could smell something too; a damp, swamp-like smell. Before the fall, he had been able to feel the tracks underneath the carriage. Now it seemed to be floating.

A figure loomed out of the darkness – a plastic model in a black cloak. But then it raised its head and David saw that it was not a model at all but a man, and a man that David knew well.

"Did you really think you could escape from us?" Mr Kilgraw asked.

The ghost train swept forward. Mrs Windergast stepped out in front of it. "I never thought you'd be so silly, my dear," she twittered.

David flinched as the carriage hurtled towards her, but at the last moment it was pulled aside by some invisible force and he found himself staring at Mr Fitch and Mr Teagle, both of them illuminated by a soft blue glow.

"A disappointment, Mr Fitch."

"A disaster, Mr Teagle."

The ghost train lurched backwards, carrying David away. Miss Pedicure waved a finger at him and tut-tutted. Monsieur Leloup, half-man, half-wolf, howled. Mr Creer, pale and semi-transparent, opened his mouth to speak but sea water flowed over his lips.

He could only sit where he was, gripping the edge of his seat, scarcely breathing as, one after another, the entire staff of Groosham Grange appeared before him. Black smoke was writhing round his feet now and he could make out a red glow in the distance, becoming brighter as he was carried towards it. Then suddenly something clanged against the back of the carriage, just above his head. He looked up. Two hands had clamped themselves against the metal, the fingers writhing. But the hands weren't attached to arms.

David yelled out.

The ghost train thundered through a second set of doors. The red glow exploded to fill his vision, a huge setting sun. A cool breeze whispered through his hair. Far below, the waves crashed against the rocks.

The ghost train had carried him back to Skrull Island. The yellow carriage was perched on the grass at the top of the cliff. There were no tracks, no models, no funfair.

It was the evening of his thirteenth birthday and the darkness of the night was closing in.

THROUGH
THE MIRROR

The school was deserted.

David had gone to bed, too depressed to do anything else. His escape had come to nothing. He had been unable to find Jill. He had just had the worst birthday of his life. And if things went the way he was expecting, it would probably also be the last.

But he couldn't sleep. Where was everybody? It had been about six o'clock when he had got back to the school. In four hours, lying in the dark, he had neither seen nor heard a soul. Not that there were any souls at Groosham Grange. They had all been sold long ago – and David knew who to.

A footfall on the bare wooden planks of the dormitory alerted him and he sat up, relaxing a moment later as Jill walked in.

"Jill!" He was relieved to see her.

"Hello, David." She sounded as depressed as he felt. "So you didn't make it?"

"I did. But ... well, it's a long story." David swung himself off the bed. He was still fully dressed. "Where is everybody?" he asked.

Jill shrugged. It was difficult to see her face. A veil of shadow had fallen over her eyes.

"What happened to you after I took the boat?" David asked.

"We can talk about that later," Jill replied. "Right now there's something I think I ought to show you. Come on!"

David followed her out of the dormitory, slightly puzzled by her. She looked well enough and he assumed that nobody had punished her for her part in the escape. But she seemed cold and distant. Perhaps she blamed him for leaving her behind. David could understand that. In a way, he still blamed himself.

"I've found out a lot of things about Groosham Grange, David," she went on as they walked down the stairs. "And a lot about the staff."

"Jill..." David reached out to stop her. "I'm sorry I had to go without you."

"That's all right, David. It all worked out for the best." She smiled at him, but her face was pale in the gloomy half-light of the hall. Breaking away, she pressed forward, moving towards the library. "All the staff here are ... well, they're not quite human. Mr Kilgraw is a vampire, Mrs Windergast is a witch. Mr Fitch and Mr Teagle are black magicians. They used to be two people until one of their experiments went wrong. Mr Creer is a ghost and Miss Pedicure has lived for ever."

"But what do they want with us?" David said.

"They want to teach us." Jill had reached the library door. She turned the handle and went in. "You're a seventh son of a seventh son. I'm a seventh daughter of a seventh daughter."

"What about it?"

"It means we're witches. We were born witches. It's not our fault. It's not anybody's fault, really. But like all the kids here we have powers. The teachers just want to show us how to use them."

"Powers?" David grabbed hold of Jill and swung her round so that she faced him. She didn't resist, but her eyes seemed to look through rather than at him. "I don't have any powers. Nor do you."

"We've got them. We just don't know how to use them." Jill was standing in front of the mirror. She reached out and rapped her knuckles against the glass. Then she turned to David. "Use your power," she challenged him.

x

148

"Go through the mirror."

"Through the glass?" David looked from the mirror to Jill and back again. He remembered his dream, how he had walked through the glass and into the underground cavern. But that had been just a dream. Now he was awake. The glass was solid. Only Jill, it seemed, had cracked.

"You can do it, David," she insisted. "You've got the power. All you have to do is use it!"

"But..."

"Try!"

Angry, confused, on the edge of fear, he wrenched himself away from her, hurling his shoulder at the glass. He would smash the mirror. That would show her. Then he would find out what was wrong with her.

His shoulder sank into the glass.

Taken by surprise, thrown off balance, David almost stumbled. His head and his raised palms made contact with the mirror – made contact with nothing – passed through the barrier as if there were no barrier at all. It was like falling into a television set. One moment he was in the library, the next he was breathing in the cold air of the tunnel, leaning against the damp and glistening rock.

He looked back the way he had come. The tunnel seemed to end with a sheet of steel. That

149

was what the mirror looked like from the other side. Then Jill stepped through it as if it were a sheet of water and stopped, her hands on her hips.

"You see," she said. "I told you you could do it."

"But how did you know about it?" David asked.

"I know a lot more..."

She brushed past him and continued down the tunnel. David followed, wondering if he was still asleep after all. But everything felt too real. He shivered in the breeze, tasted the salt water on his lips, felt the weight of the rocks hemming him in. The passage dipped down and his ears popped as the pressure increased.

"Where does this lead to?" he asked.

"You'll see."

When it seemed that they had walked half a mile, David became aware of a strange, silver glow. There had been no light bulbs or torches to light the way and he realized now that the tunnel had been filled with the same silvery glow as if it were a mist rising from a subterranean lake. Jill stopped, waiting for him to catch up. He hurried forward, out of the tunnel and into...

It was a huge cavern, the cavern of his dream. Stalactites and stalagmites hung down, soared up, as if carved from the dreams of Nature itself. One entire wall was covered by a petrified waterfall, brilliant white, a frozen eternity. In the middle of it all stood the sacrificial block, solid granite, horribly final. Mr Kilgraw was standing behind it. He had been waiting for them. Jill had led him to them.

David spun round, searching for something he knew he would find, something he should have seen from the start. And there it was, on her third finger. A black ring.

"Jill...!" He shook his head, unable to speak. "When were you thirteen?" he demanded at last.

"Yesterday," Jill said. She looked at him reproachfully. "You never wished me a happy birthday. But I don't mind, David." She smiled. "You see, we were wrong. We were fighting them. But all the time they were really on our side."

The despair was like quicksand, sucking him in. There was no more fight in him. He had failed – failed to escape, failed to do anything. Jill had been taken. She was one of them. At last he was finally alone.

And now it was his turn.

They had come for him.

As one, the pupils of Groosham Grange moved out of the shadows at the edge of the cavern, forming a circle around him. The rest of the staff appeared behind Mr Kilgraw. David walked slowly to the granite block. He didn't want to walk there. But his legs would no longer obey his commands.

He stopped in front of Mr Kilgraw. The other pupils had closed the circle, locking him in. Everyone was looking at him.

"You have fought us long and hard, David," Mr Kilgraw said. "I congratulate you on your courage. But the time for fighting is over. Today is your thirteenth birthday. Midnight is approaching. You must make your choice.

"Listen to me, David. You are the seventh son of a seventh son. That is why you were brought to Groosham Grange. You have powers. We want to teach you how to use them."

"I'm not a witch!" David cried. The words echoed around the cavern. "I never will be!"

"Why not?" Mr Kilgraw had not raised his voice but he was speaking with an intensity and a passion that David had never heard before. "Why not, David? Why do you refuse to see things our way? You think ghosts and witches and vampires and ghosts and two-headed monsters are bad. Why? Do you know what that is, David? It's prejudice. Racial prejudice!"

Mr Fitch and Mr Teagle nodded appreciatively. Mrs Windergast muttered a brief "Hear! Hear!"

"There's nothing bad about us. Have we hurt

152

you? True, we had to see to Mr Netherby, but that was no fault of ours. You brought him here. We were only protecting ourselves.

"The trouble is, you've seen too many horror films. We vampires have never had a fair deal on the screen. And look at werewolves! Just because my good friend Monsieur Leloup likes the occasional pigeon salad when there's a full moon, everyone thinks they've a right to hunt him down and shoot silver bullets in him. And what about Mr Creer? All right, so he's dead. But he's still a very good teacher – in fact, he's a lot more lively than quite a few living teachers I could mention."

"But I'm not like you," David insisted. "I don't want to be like you."

"You have power," Mr Kilgraw replied. "That is all that matters. And the real question you should be asking yourself, David, is, do you really want to stay with your parents and follow your singularly unpleasant father into merchant banking? Or do you want to be free?

"Join us, and you'll be rich. We can teach you how to make gold out of lead, how to destroy your enemies just by snapping your fingers. We can show you how to see into the future and use it for yourself. Think of it, David! You can have everything you want ... and more. Look at Miss Pedicure! She's lived for ever. So can you...

153

"All right, I admit it. We are, frankly, evil. My friends Mr Fitch and Mr Teagle are more evil than any of us. They've won awards for being evil. But what's so bad about being evil? *We've* never dropped an atom bomb on anyone. *We've* never polluted the environment or experimented on animals or cut back on National Health spending. Our evil is rather agreeable. Why do you think there have been so many books and films about us? It's because people like us. We are actually rather pleasantly evil."

While Mr Kilgraw had spoken, the sixty-four pupils of Groosham Grange, novice witches and young adepts all, had tightened the circle. Now they were moving closer to David, their eyes bearing down on him. Jill was next to Jeffrey. William Rufus was on the other side. Sixty-four black rings glowed in the underground light.

Mr Kilgraw held the sixty-fifth.

"I have enjoyed the fight, David," he said. "I didn't want it to be easy. I admire courage. But now it is midnight." He reached out with his other hand. Gregor scurried forward and gave him his knife.

"Here is your choice," he went on. "The ring or the knife? You can reject us one final time. In that instance, I regret that I will be forced to plunge the blade into your heart. I can assure you that it will hurt me more than it will hurt you. And we'll give you a decent burial in the school cemetery.

"Alternatively, you can accept us, take a new name and begin your education in earnest. But there can be no going back, David. If you join us, you join us for ever."

David felt himself being forced down on to the granite block. The circle of faces spun round him. There was the ring. And there was the knife.

"Now, David," Mr Kilgraw asked. "What do you say?"

SEVENTH SON

"When I was a boy," Mr Eliot said, "I had to work in my holidays. My father made me work so hard I'd have to spend three weeks in hospital before I could go back to school."

"But David's only got one day's holiday," Mrs Eliot reminded him, pouring herself a glass of gin.

"I am aware of that, my dear." Mr Eliot snatched the glass out of her hand and drank it himself. "And if you ask me, one day is much too long. If I'd been expelled from Beton College my father would never have spoken to me again. In fact he'd have cut off my ears so I wouldn't hear him if he spoke to me accidentally."

The two parents were sitting in the living-room of their house in Wiernotta Mews. Edward Eliot was smoking a cigar. Eileen Eliot was stroking Beefeater, her favourite Siamese cat. They had just eaten lunch – ham salad served in true vegetarian style, without the ham.

"Maybe we should take him to a film or something?" Mrs Eliot suggested nervously.

"A film?"

"Well ... or a concert..."

"Are you mad?" Mr Eliot snapped. He leant forward angrily and stubbed his cigar out on the cat. The cat screeched and leapt off Mrs Eliot, its back claws ripping off most of her stockings and part of her leg. "Why should we take him anywhere?" Mr Eliot demanded.

"Perhaps you are right, my love," Mrs Eliot whimpered, pouring the rest of the gin on to her leg to stop the bleeding.

Just then the door opened and David walked in.

He had changed since his departure for Groosham Grange. He was thinner, older, somehow wiser. He had always been quiet. But now there was something strange about his silence. It was like a wall between him and his parents. And when he looked at them, it was with soft, almost merciless, eyes.

Mr Eliot glanced at his watch. "Well, David," he said. "You've got seven hours and twenty-two minutes before your holiday's over. So why don't you go and mow the lawn?"

"But it's a plastic lawn!" Mrs Eliot protested.

"Then he can go and wash it!"

"Of course, dear!" Mrs Eliot beamed at her husband, then fainted from loss of blood.

David sighed. Seven hours and twenty-two minutes. He hadn't realized there was still so much time.

He lifted his right hand.

"What's that you're wearing?" his father demanded.

David muttered a few words under his breath.

There was no puff of smoke, no flash of light. But it was as if his parents had been photographed and at the same time turned into those photographs. Mrs Eliot was halfway out of her chair, slumping towards the carpet. Mr Eliot was about to speak, his mouth open, his tongue hovering over his teeth.

It was a simple spell. But they would remain that way for the next three weeks.

David rubbed his black ring thoughtfully. He had spoken the words of power with perfect pronunciation. Mrs Windergast would have said that three weeks was overdoing it when a few hours would have been enough, but then she was a perfectionist and all David's spells tended to be on the strong side. Maybe he was just a little enthusiastic.

He went upstairs and lay down on his bed.

A chocolate milk shake materialized in thin air and began to float towards him. He was looking forward to the next term at Groosham Grange. He and Jill would both be taking their first GCSEs in the summer: Telepathy, Weather Control, Wax Modelling and (the trickiest of the four) Advanced Blood Sacrifice.

And what then? He sipped the milk shake and smiled. He'd got it exactly right – thick with plenty of chocolate. He still blushed when he remembered his first attempt. In cookery class he'd conjured up a perfect milk shake: banana flavour with two scoops of ice-cream. But he'd forgotten to include a glass. It was only recently that he'd got used to his powers, begun to enjoy them.

So what would he do with them? Black magic or white magic? Good or evil?

He would leave that decision until later – at least until he'd passed his exams. And David was certain that he would pass. He was the seventh son of a seventh son. And he had never felt better in his life.

RETURN TO GROOSHAM GRANGE

ANTHONY HOROWITZ

TOP SECRET

To The Right Reverend Morris Grope
Bishop of Bletchley

Dear Bishop,

I have now been at Groosham Grange for three months. I've had a terrible time. The teachers here are all monsters. The children are evil ... and worse still, they enjoy being evil. They even get prizes for it! I hate having to pretend that I like it here, but of course it's the only way to be sure that nobody finds out who I really am.

But all the time I'm thinking about my mission, the reason you sent me here. You wanted me to find a way to destroy the school and the island on which it stands. And the good news is that I think it can be done. At last I have found a way.

It seems that all the power of Groosham

Grange is concentrated in a silver cup. They call this cup the Unholy Grail. It's kept hidden in a cave — nobody can get close to it. But once a year it's taken out and given as a prize to the boy or girl who has come top in the school exams. This will happen just a few weeks from now.

I've also been doing some research. Looking in the school library, I found an old book of sorcery and spells. In the very back there was a poem. This is what it said:

BEWARE THE SHADOW THAT IS FOUND
STRETCHING OUT ACROSS THE GROUND
WHERE ST AUGUSTINE ONCE BEGAN
AND FOUR KNIGHTS SLEW A HOLY MAN
FOR IF THE GRAIL IS CARRIED HERE
THEN GROOSHAM GRANGE WILL DISAPPEAR

And now the good news, your Holiness! I've worked out what the poem means. And if I can get my hands on the Grail, then I will have

accomplished my mission and Groosham Grange
will be no more.

With best wishes to you and to Mrs Grope,

Your obedient servant,

secret agent at Groosham Grange

SPORTS DAY

It was Sports Day at Groosham Grange – the egg and spoon race – and the egg was winning. It was running on long, elegant legs while the spoon struggled to keep up. In another corner of the field, the three-legged race had just been won, for the second year running, by a boy with three legs, while the parents' race had been cancelled when someone remembered that none of the parents had actually been invited.

There had been one unfortunate incident during the afternoon. Gregor, the school porter, had been disqualified from javelin-throwing. He had strolled across the pitch without looking and although he hadn't actually entered the competition, one of the javelins had unfortunately entered him. Mrs Windergast, the school matron, had taken him to the sick-bay with two metres of aluminium jutting out of his shoulder, but it was only when he got there that she had discovered that he couldn't actually get through the door.

Otherwise everything had gone smoothly. The teachers' race had been won, for the third year running, by Mr Kilgraw (dressed in protective black clothing) and Mr Creer. As one was a vampire and the other a ghost it was hardly surprising that the race always ended in a dead heat. At four o'clock, the high jump was followed by a high tea: traditionally it was served on the school battlements.

If anyone had happened to see the sixty-five boys and girls gathered together along with their seven teachers around the sandwiches and strawberries and cream they would have thought this was an ordinary sports day at an ordinary school ... even if the building itself did look a little like Frankenstein's castle. Looking closer, they might have been puzzled by the fact that everyone in the school was wearing, as well as their sports kit, an identical black ring. But it would only be if they happened to catch sight of Mr Fitch and Mr Teagle, the two heads of Groosham Grange, that they might begin to guess the truth.

For the heads of the school were just that. Two heads on one body: the result of an experiment that had gone horribly wrong. Mr Teagle, bearded and wearing a boater, was eating a cucumber with a pinch of salt. Mr Fitch, bald and hatless, was chewing a triangle of bread with a little butter. And the two men were both enjoying what would be a perfect sandwich by the time it disappeared down the same, single throat.

Of course, Groosham Grange was anything but ordinary. As well as the ghost, the vampire and the head with two heads, the other teachers included a werewolf, a witch and a three-thousand-year-old woman. All the children there were the seventh sons of seventh sons and the seventh daughters of seventh daughters. They had been born with magical powers and the school's real purpose was to teach them how to use those powers in the outside world.

"So what's the last race?" Mr Teagle asked, helping himself to a cocktail sausage. The wrinkled sausage at the end of its long wooden stick somehow reminded him of Gregor after his recent accident.

"The obstacle race," Mr Fitch replied.

"Ah yes! Good, good. And who are the finalists?"

Mr Fitch took a sip of plain, black tea. "William Rufus. Jill Green. Jeffrey Joseph. Vincent King. And David Eliot."

Mr Teagle popped two sugar-lumps and a

spoonful of milk into his mouth. "David Eliot. That should be interesting."

Ten minutes later, David stood on the starting line, surveying the course ahead. The obstacle race would be, he was certain, like no other obstacle race in the world. And he was equally certain that he would win it.

He had been at Groosham Grange for almost a year. In that time he had grown six inches, filled out a bit so he looked less like a street urchin, more like a sprinter. He wore his brown hair long now, thrown back off a face that had become paler and more serious. His blue-green eyes had become guarded, almost secretive.

But the real changes had been happening inside him. He had hated the school when he had first arrived ... but that had been before he had discovered why he was there. Now he accepted it. He was the seventh son of a seventh son. That was how he had been born and there was nothing he could do about it. It seemed incredible to him that once he had fought against the school and tried to escape from it. Today, a year later, he knew that there was nowhere else he would rather be. He belonged here. And in just two weeks' time he knew he would walk away with the school's top prize: the Unholy Grail.

There was a movement beside him and he

turned to see a tall, fair-haired boy with square shoulders and a smiling, handsome face, walking up to the starting line. Vincent King was the newest arrival at Groosham Grange. He had only come to the school three months before, but in that time he had made astonishing progress. From the moment the school's secrets had been revealed to him and he had been awarded his black ring, he had surged ahead and, although David was well ahead in the school exams, there were some who said that Vincent could still catch up.

Maybe this was one of the reasons why David didn't like the other boy. The two of them had been in competition from the very start, but recently the sense of competitiveness had bubbled over into something else. David mistrusted Vincent. He wasn't sure why. And he was determined to beat him.

David watched as Vincent stretched himself, preparing for the race. Neither of them spoke to each other. It had been a while since they had been on talking terms. At the same time, Jill Green strolled over to them. Jill was David's best friend – the two of them had arrived at the school on the same day – and he was annoyed to see her smile at Vincent.

"Good luck," she said.

"Thanks." Vincent smiled back.

David opened his mouth to say something but then Jeffrey and William arrived and he realized it was time to take his place on the starting line. Mr Kilgraw – who taught Latin – appeared, carrying a starting pistol in his black-gloved hand. The rest of the school were standing a short distance away, watching.

"Take your places," the Latin teacher said.

He raised the gun.

"Sistite! Surgite! Currite...!" *

He fired. Two hundred metres above him, a crow squawked and plunged to the ground. The race had begun.

The five runners set off along the course, racing down the green to the first obstacle – a net hanging thirty metres high from a wooden frame. Jeffrey had taken an early lead, but David was amused to see him make his first mistake and start climbing the net. For his part, he muttered a quick spell and levitated himself over it. William and Jill turned themselves into dragonflies and flew through it. Vincent had dematerialized and reappeared on the other side. The four of them were neck and neck.

The second obstacle in the race was a shallow pit filled with burning coals. All the children had studied Hawaiian fire-walking and David didn't even hesitate. He took the pit in eight strides, noticing out of the corner of his eye that

*Ready, steady, go!

William had forgotten to tie one of his shoelaces and had set light to his Nike trainer. That left three.

With the cheers of the rest of the school urging them on, David, Jill and Vincent twisted round the oak-tree at the end of the course and disappeared completely. How typical of Mr Creer to sneak a dimensional warp into the race! One second David was running past the tree with the cliffs ahead of him and the grass swaying gently in the breeze, the next he was battling through a cyclonic storm of wind and poisonous gases on a planet somewhere on the other side of the universe. It had to be Jupiter from the look of it. Sixteen moons hung in the night sky over him and the gravity was so intense that he could barely lift his feet. The smell of ammonium hydrosulphide made his eyes water and he was glad that he had reacted quickly enough to remember to hold his breath.

He could hear Jill catching up with him, her feet scrunching on the orange and grey rubble of the planet's surface. Glancing quickly over his shoulder, he also saw Vincent, rapidly gaining ground. He staggered past the remains of a NASA space probe, heading for a flag that had been planted about a hundred metres away. His teeth were already chattering – the planet was freezing cold – and he cried out as he was hit by a primordial gas cloud that completely blinded him. But then he was aware that there was grass under his feet once again and, opening his eyes, he saw that he was back on Skrull Island. He had passed the third obstacle. The finishing line was ahead. But there were still three more challenges before he got there.

He looked back. Jeffrey and William were far behind. Vincent had overtaken Jill and was only about twenty metres away. With his attention on the other boy, David almost ran straight into the giant spider's web that was the next obstacle. It had been spun between two trees, almost invisible until you were in it and David had to twist desperately to avoid the threads. Even so, a single strand – thick and sticky – caught his arm and he had to waste precious seconds tearing it free. Somehow, though, he managed to get through. He tumbled to the ground, somersaulted forward, then got up and ran.

"Come on, Vincent! You can do it!"

David knew that there were as many people cheering him as there were Vincent. But it still irritated him to hear Vincent's name being called out by his friends. His anger spurred him on and he easily cleared the six hurdles ahead of him without even thinking about the ten thousand volts of electricity to which they were connected. That just left the bottomless pit with two narrow planks to carry the runners on to the end.

His foot hit the left plank. It was less than six centimetres wide and bent slightly as it took his weight. David swayed as he fought to regain his balance and that was when he made his second mistake. He looked down. The pit ran all the way through the centre of the earth and out the other side. One slip and he would find himself in New Zealand. David had never been fond of heights and right now he was suspended over what looked like an impossible lift shaft, though without the advantage of a lift. Again he had to waste time fighting off the rush of dizziness and nausea. And that was when Vincent overtook him.

David didn't even see the other boy. He was aware only of a shape rushing past him on the other plank. Biting his lip, he forced himself forward. Ten steps, the wooden surface bouncing and bending underneath him, and then he had reached the other side with Vincent between him and the finishing line. Meanwhile, Jill had caught up. She had taken the same plank as him and she was so close that he could almost feel her breath on the back of his neck.

With one last effort, David pushed ahead. The red tape that would end the race was fifty metres ahead. Vincent was just in front of him. The cheering spectators were on both sides, Mr

Kilgraw holding a stopwatch, Mr Fitch and Mr Teagle applauding and Mrs Windergast giving mouth-to-mouth to the injured crow.

David didn't know what he was going to do until he did it. He was still holding the strand of spider's web and with a flick of his hand he threw it in front of him. Even if anyone had been close enough to see what he had done, it might have looked like an accident, as if he had just been trying to get rid of it. The piece of web twisted round Vincent's left ankle and hooked itself over his right foot. It wasn't enough to stop him but it made him stumble and at that exact moment David overtook him and with a final gasp felt the tape of the finishing line break over his chest.

It was over. He had won.

The entire school went crazy. Everyone was yelling now. David collapsed on to the soft grass and rolled on to his back, while the clouds, the people and the fluttering tape spun around him. Vincent thudded to a halt, his hands on his thighs, panting. Jill had come in third, William fourth. Jeffrey had managed to get himself stuck in the web and was still hanging in the air some distance behind.

"Well done, David!" Mr Creer was standing by the finishing line with a ghost of a smile on his lips. But all his smiles were quite naturally ghostly. "Well run!"

David had beaten Vincent, but he felt no pleasure. As he got to his feet, he was ashamed of himself. He had cheated in front of the entire school, he knew it, and it only made him feel worse when Vincent came over to him with an outstretched hand.

"Good race," Vincent said.

"Thanks." David took the hand, wishing he could undo what he had just done but knowing that it was too late.

He turned to find Jill looking at him strangely. Of course, she had been closest to him when it happened. If anyone could have seen what he'd done, it would have been her. But what would she do? Would she tell?

"Jill…" he began.

But she had already turned her back on him and now she walked away.

ON THE ROCKS

David was sitting on a long, rocky outcrop, with the cliffs rising up behind him and the sea lapping at his feet. It was one of his favourite places on Skrull Island. He loved the sound of the waves, the emptiness of the horizon, with the great bulk of the Norfolk coastline a grey haze somewhere beyond. He would sit here with the wind rushing at his cheeks and the taste of sea-spray on his lips. This was where he came to think.

Twenty-four hours had passed since Sports Day and the excitement of the obstacle race, and in all that time his mood hadn't changed. He was depressed, disappointed with himself. There had been no need to win the race. There were no prizes or cups given out on Sports Day. So what reason did he have to cheat?

"Vincent King..." he muttered to himself.

"What about him?"

He looked round and saw Jill Green walking towards him. She had changed as much as he had in the year she had been at Groosham Grange. She was quieter, more relaxed ... and prettier. With her long dark hair and pale skin, she looked rather like a young witch, which was, of course, exactly what she was.

She sat down next to him. "I can't believe what you did yesterday," she said.

"You saw..."

"Yes."

"I was stupid." David was glad she had brought up the subject even though he was almost too ashamed to talk about it. "I didn't mean to do it." He sighed. "But I couldn't let him win. I just couldn't. I don't know why."

"You don't like him."

"No."

"But why not? Vincent's bright. He's popular. And he's very good-looking."

"That's why I don't like him," David said. He thought for a minute. "He's too perfect altogether. If you ask me, there's something funny about him."

"And if you ask me," Jill said, "you're just jealous."

"Jealous?" David picked up a loose stone and threw it into the sea. He waited until it had disappeared, then reached out with one hand. The stone rocketed out of the water and slapped itself back into his palm. He handed it to Jill.

"Very clever," she muttered, sourly.

"Why should I be jealous of Vincent?" David said. "If you're talking about the Unholy Grail, he hasn't got a chance."

"He's only thirty points behind you. He could still catch up."

There were just two weeks until 31 October – Hallowe'en – the most important day in the school's calendar. For this was when the Unholy Grail would be presented to the new Student Master. Throughout the year, all the marks from all the exams had been added up and published on a league table which hung on a wall outside the heads' study. David had been top of the league from the start.

But Vincent had risen so fast that his name was now only one below David's and, although everyone agreed the distance between them was too great, nothing was ever certain, particularly in a school like Groosham Grange. There was, after all, one exam still to go – Advanced Cursing. And David had to remember, it was also possible to lose marks. You could have them deducted for bad behaviour, for being late ... and for being caught cheating in a sports day race.

"Do you like him?" David asked.

"Yes."

"Do you fancy him?"

"That's none of your business." Jill sighed. "Why are you so bothered about him?"

"I don't know." David shivered. The waves were whispering to him, he was sure of it. But he couldn't understand what they were saying. His hand felt cold where it had touched the stone. "There's something wrong about him," he said. "Something phoney. I can feel it."

In the distance, a bell rang. It was a quarter to four, almost time for the last two lessons of the day: French with Monsieur Leloup, then general witchcraft with Mrs Windergast. David wasn't looking forward to the French. He was almost fluent in Latin and spoke passable Ancient Egyptian, but he couldn't understand the point of learning modern languages. "After all," he often said, "I can summon up fourteen demons and two demi-gods in Egyptian, but what can I ask for in French? A plate of cheese!" Nonetheless, Groosham Grange insisted on teaching the full range of GCSE and A level subjects as well as its own more specialized ones. And there were serious punishments if you travelled forward in time just to miss the next lesson.

"We'd better move," he said.

Jill took hold of his arm. "David," she said. "Promise me you won't cheat again. I mean, it's not like you…"

David looked straight into her eyes. "I promise."

Ahead of them, Groosham Grange rose into sight. Even after a year on the island, David still found the school building rather grim. Sometimes it looked like a castle, sometimes more like a haunted house. At night, with the moon sinking behind its great towers to the east and west, it could have been an asylum for the criminally insane. The windows were barred, the doors so thick that when they slammed you could hear them a mile away. And yet David liked it – that was the strange thing. Once it had been new and strange and frightening. Now it was his home.

"Are your parents coming?" Jill asked.

"What?"

"In two weeks' time. For prize-giving."

David had hardly seen Edward and Eileen Eliot since the day he had started at Groosham Grange. Parents very rarely came to the school. But as it happened, he had received a letter from his father just a few days before:

Dear David,

This is to inform you that your mother and I will be visiting Groosham Grange for prize-giving on 31 October. We will also be bringing my sister, your Aunt Mildred, and

180

will then drive her home to Margate. This means that I will be spending only half the day at the school. To save time, I am also sending you only half a letter.

And that was where it ended. The page had been torn neatly in two.

"Yes. They're coming," David said. "How about yours?"

"No." Jill shook her head. Her father was a diplomat and her mother an actress, so she hardly ever saw either of them. "Dad's in Argentina and Mum's acting in *The Cherry Orchard*."

"Has she got a good part?"

"She's playing one of the cherries."

They had reached the school now. Jill glanced at her watch. "It's two minutes to four," she said. "We're going to be late."

"You go ahead," David muttered.

"Cheer up, David." Jill started forward, then turned her head. "You're probably right. You'll win the Grail. There's nothing to worry about."

David watched her go, then turned off, making his way round the East Tower and on through the school's own private cemetery. It was a short cut he often used. But now, just as he reached the first grave, he stopped. Before he knew what he was doing he had crouched down behind a gravestone, all other thoughts having emptied out of his head.

Slowly, he peered over the top. A door had opened at the side of the school. There was nothing strange about that except that the door was always locked. It led into a small antechamber in the East Tower. From there a stone staircase spiralled two hundred metres up to a completely circular room at the top. Nobody ever went into the East Tower. There was nothing downstairs and the old, crumbling stairway was supposedly too dangerous to climb. The whole place was out of bounds. But somebody was about to come out. Who?

A few seconds later the question was answered as a boy stepped out, looking cautiously about him. David recognized him at once: his blond hair thrown back in a fancy wave across his forehead and his piercing blue eyes, which were now narrow and guarded. Vincent King had been up to something in the East Tower and he didn't want anyone to know about it. Without turning back, he pulled the door shut behind him, then hurried away in the direction of the school.

David waited a few moments before rising from behind the gravestone. He was going to be late for his French lesson and he knew it would get him into trouble but his curiosity had got the better of him. What had Vincent been doing inside? He started forward. The tower rose up in front of him, half strangled by the ivy that twisted around it. He could just make out the slit of a window beneath the battlements. Was it just a trick of the light or was something moving behind it? Had Vincent been meeting someone high up in the circular room?

He reached out for the door.

But then a hand clamped down on his shoulder, spinning him round as somebody lurched at him, appearing from nowhere. David caught his breath. Then he relaxed. It was only Gregor, the school porter.

Even so, anyone else being stopped by such a creature on the edge of a cemetery would probably have had a heart attack. Gregor was like something out of a horror film, his neck broken and his skin like mouldy cheese. At least the javelin had been removed from his back, although he evidently hadn't changed his shirt. David could still see the hole where the javelin had gone in.

"Vareyoo goink, young master?" Gregor asked in his strange, gurgling voice. Gregor chewed on his words like raw meat. He also chewed raw meat. His table manners were so disgusting that he was usually made to eat under the table.

"I was just..." David wasn't sure what to say.

"Butzee lessons, young master. Yoom issink zee lovely lessons. You shoot be hurryink in."

Gregor moved so that he stood between David and the door to the tower.

"Hold on, Gregor," David began. "I just need a few minutes…"

"No minutes." Gregor lurched from one foot to the other, his hands hanging down to his knees. "Is bad marks for missink lessons. And too many bad marks and there izno Unnerly Grail for the young master. Yes! Gregor knows…"

"What do you know, Gregor?" Suddenly David was suspicious. It was almost as if Gregor had been waiting for him at the tower. Had he seen Vincent coming out? And why had he suddenly mentioned the Grail? There was certainly more to this than met the eye … which, in Gregor's case, was about three centimetres below his other eye.

"Hurry, young master," Gregor insisted.

"All right," David said. "I'm going." He turned his back on the porter and walked quickly towards his classroom. But now he was certain. He had been listening to the voice of his sixth sense when he was down on the rocks – and hadn't Groosham Grange taught him that the sixth sense was much more important than the other five?

Something was going on at the school. In some way it was connected to the Unholy Grail. And whatever it was, David was going to find out.

FLYING LESSON

David opened the classroom door nervously. He was ten minutes late, which was bad enough, but this was French with Monsieur Leloup, which was worse. Monsieur Leloup had a bad temper – hardly surprising considering he was a werewolf. Even on a good day he had been known to rip a French dictionary to pieces with his teeth. On a bad day, when there was going to be a full moon, he had to be chained to his desk in case he did the same to his class.

Fortunately, the full moon had been and gone but even so, David walked gingerly into the room. His empty desk stared accusingly at him in the middle of all the others. Just as he reached it, Monsieur Leloup turned from the blackboard.

"You are late, Monsieur Eliot," he snapped.

"I'm sorry, sir..." David said.

"Ten minutes late. Can you tell me where you have been?"

David opened his mouth to speak, then thought better of it. He could see Vincent out of the corner of his eye. Vincent had the desk behind his. He was pretending to read his book but there was a half smile on his lips, as if he knew what was going to happen. "I was just out walking," David said.

"Walking?" Monsieur Leloup sniffed. "I shall deduct three marks from the league table. Now will you please take your seat. We are discussing the future perfect..."

David sat down and opened his book. He had got off lightly and he knew it. Three marks deducted still left him twenty-seven ahead. There was no way Vincent could catch up, no matter what happened in the last exam. He was fine.

Even so, David concentrated more than usual for the next fifty minutes just in case he was asked something, and he was relieved when the bell rang at five o'clock and the lesson was over.

He joined the general stream out of the class and down the corridor to the last lesson of the day. He found this one a lot more interesting: general witchcraft, taught by Mrs Windergast. Even after a year at the school, David still hadn't quite got used to the matron's methods. Only a week before he had gone to her with a headache and she had given him not an aspirin but an asp. She had fished the small, slithering snake out of a glass jar and held it against his head ... an example of what she called sympathetic magic. David had found it a rather unnerving experience – although he'd been forced to admit that it worked.

Today she was discussing the power of flight. And she wasn't talking about aeroplanes.

"The broomstick was always the favoured vehicle of the sisterhood," she was saying. "Can anyone tell me what it was made of?"

A girl in the front row put up her hand. "Hazel wood?"

"Quite right, Linda. Hazel wood is the correct answer. Now, who can tell me why some people believe that witches used to keep cats?"

The same girl put up her hand. "Because 'cat' was the old word for broomstick," she volunteered.

"Right again, Linda." Mrs Windergast muttered a few words. There was a flash of light and, with a little shriek, Linda exploded. All that was left of her was a puddle of slime and a few strands of hair. "It is never wise to know all the answers," Mrs Windergast remarked, acidly. "To answer once is fine. To answer twice is showing off. I hope Linda will have learned that now."

Mrs Windergast smiled. She was a small, round woman who looked like the perfect grand-mother. But in fact she was lethal. She had been burned at the stake in 1214 (during the reign of King John) and again in 1336. Not surprisingly, she now tended to keep herself to herself and she never went to barbecues.

"Linda was, however, quite right," she continued. She pulled a broomstick out from behind the blackboard. "Witches never had cats. It was just a misunderstanding. This is my own 'cat' and today I want to show you how difficult it is to control. Would anyone like to try it?"

Nobody moved. All eyes were on Linda's empty desk and the green smoke still curling above it.

Mrs Windergast pointed. "Vincent King..."

Vincent stood up and moved to the front of the classroom. David's eyes narrowed. Mrs Windergast was obviously in a bad mood today. Maybe Vincent would say something to annoy her and go the same way as Linda. Or was that too much to hope?

"My broomstick is very precious to me," Mrs Windergast was saying. "I normally keep it very close to me – as do all witches. So this is very much an honour, young man. Do you think you could ride it?"

"Yeah – I think so."

"Then try."

Vincent took hold of the broomstick and muttered some words of power. At once the stick sprang to attention and hovered in the air, a few metres above the ground. Gracefully, he climbed on to it, swinging one leg over it as if it were a horse. David watched, annoyed and showing it. It seemed there was nothing Vincent couldn't do well. He had both feet off the ground now, hovering in space as if he had been born to it.

"Try moving," Mrs Windergast suggested.

Vincent concentrated and slowly rose into the air, perfectly balanced on the broomstick. Gently he curved round and headed over the blackboard, the handle ahead of him, the twigs trailing behind. He was smiling, growing in confidence, and David was half tempted to whisper the spell that would summon up a minor wind-demon and knock him off balance.

But in the end there was no need. When things went wrong they all went wrong at once. The broomstick wobbled, the end pitched up, Vincent cried out and the next moment he fell off and crashed to the floor with the broom on top of him.

"As you can see," Mrs Windergast trilled, "it's not as easy as it looks. Is there any damage,

Vincent dear?"

Vincent got stiffly to his feet, rubbing his shoulder. "I'm all right," he said.

"I meant the broomstick." Mrs Windergast picked it up and cast a fond eye over it. "I never let anyone ride it as a rule," she went on. "But it seems undamaged. Well done, Vincent. You may return to your seat. And now..." She turned to the blackboard, "...let me try to explain the curious mixture of magic and basic aerodynamics that makes flight possible."

For the next forty-five minutes, Mrs Windergast explained her technique. David was sorry when the final bell went. He had enjoyed the lesson – Vincent's fall in particular – and he was still smiling as he left the classroom. Linda followed him out. She had been reconstituted by Mrs Windergast but she was looking very pale and sickly. David doubted if she would ever make a decent black magician. She'd probably end up as nothing worse than a traffic warden.

There was a knot of people outside in the corridor. As David came out he saw that one of them was Vincent.

"That was bad luck," Vincent said.

"What?" Maybe it was just an innocent remark but already David felt his hackles rise.

"Losing three marks in French. That narrows the gap."

"You're still a long way behind." It was Jill who had spoken. David hadn't seen her arrive but he was glad that she seemed to have taken his side.

"The exams haven't finished yet." Vincent shrugged and once again David was irritated without knowing why. Did he dislike Vincent just because he was his closest rival or was there something more? Looking at his easy smile, the way Vincent slouched against the wall – always so superior – he felt something snap inside.

"You looked pretty stupid just now," he said.

"When?"

"Falling off the broomstick."

"You think you could have done better?"

"Sure." David wasn't thinking. All he knew was that he wanted to goad the other boy, just to get a reaction. "You're going to have to get used to coming second," he went on. "Just like in the race..."

Vincent's eyes narrowed. He took a step forward. "There was only one reason I came second..." he began.

He knew what David had done. He had felt the web slipping over his foot. And he was going to say it, now, in front of everyone. David couldn't let that happen. He had to stop him. And before he knew what he was doing, he suddenly reached out and pushed Vincent hard

191

with the heel of his hand. Vincent was taken off balance and cried out as his bruised shoulder hit the wall behind him.

"David!" Jill cried out.

She was too late. Without hesitating, Vincent bounced back, throwing himself on to David. David's books and papers were torn out of his hands and scattered across the floor. Vincent was taller, heavier and stronger than him. But even as he felt the other boy's hand on his throat he couldn't help feeling pleased with himself. He had wanted to get past Vincent's defences and he'd done it. He'd taken the upper hand.

Right now, though, Vincent's upper hand was slowly strangling him. David brought up his knee, felt it sink into Vincent's stomach. Vincent grunted and twisted hard. David's head cracked against the panelling.

"What's going on here? Stop it at once!"

David's heart sank. Of all the people who could have happened along the corridor just then, Mr Helliwell was unquestionably the worst. He was a huge man with wide shoulders and a round, bald head. He had only recently joined the school, teaching arts and crafts by day and voodoo by night. He came from Haiti where he was apparently so feared as a magician that people actually fainted if he said "Good morning" to them and for six months the postman had been too scared to deliver the mail – which didn't matter too much as nobody on the island was brave enough to write. David had somehow found himself on the wrong side of Mr Helliwell from the very start and this was only going to make things worse.

"David? Vincent?" The teacher looked from one to the other. "Who started this?"

David hesitated. He was blushing and it was only now that he realized how stupid he had been. He had behaved like an ordinary boy at an ordinary school. At Groosham Grange, there was no worse crime. "It was me," he admitted.

Vincent looked at him but said nothing. Jill and the other onlookers seemed to have vanished. There were just the three of them left in the corridor. Mr Helliwell glanced down at the floor. He leant forward, picked up a sheet of paper and quickly read it. He handed it to David. "This is yours."

David took it. It was the letter from his father.

"You started the fight?" Mr Helliwell asked.

"Yes," David said.

Mr Helliwell considered. His grey eyes gave nothing away. "Very well," he said. "This is going to cost you nine marks. And if I see you behaving like this again, I'll send you to the heads."

Mr Helliwell turned and walked away. David watched him go, then leant down and picked up the rest of his books and papers. He could feel Vincent watching him. He glanced up.

Vincent shrugged. "Don't blame me," he said.

And then he was on his own. In one afternoon he had lost an incredible twelve marks! His lead had gone down by almost half – from thirty to eighteen. At lunch-time he had been right at the top of the league table, secure, unassailable. But now...

David gritted his teeth. There was only one more exam to go. It was his best subject. And he was still a long way ahead of Vincent. The Unholy Grail would be his.

Scooping up the last of his books, David set off down the empty corridor, the sound of his own footsteps echoing around him.

FRAMED

That night David had a bad dream.

Vincent King was part of it, of course. Vincent laughing at him. Vincent holding the Unholy Grail. Vincent slipping out of the East Tower and disappearing like a wisp of smoke into one of the graves.

But there were other, more frightening things woven into the night canvas. First there were his parents – only they weren't his parents. They were changing, transforming into something horrible. And then there was a face that he knew, looming over him. He would have been able to recognize it but he was lying on his back, in pain, blinded by a fiery sun. And finally he saw the school, Groosham Grange, standing stark against a darkening sky. As he watched, a bolt of lightning streaked down and smashed into it. A great crack appeared in the stonework. Dust and rubble exploded out.

And that was when he woke up.

There were nine dormitories at Groosham Grange. The one that David slept in was completely circular with the beds arranged like numbers on a clock-face. Vincent had been put in the same room as him, his bed opposite David's, underneath a window. Propping himself up on one elbow, David could see the other boy's bed, clearly illuminated by a shaft of moonlight flooding in from above. It was empty.

Where could Vincent be? David glanced at the chair beside Vincent's bed. Wherever he had gone, he had taken his clothes with him. Outside, a clock struck four. At almost exactly the same moment, David heard a door creak open somewhere below and then swing shut. It had to be Vincent. Nobody else would be up and about in the middle of the night. David threw back the covers and got out of bed. He would find out what was going on.

He got dressed quickly and crept out of the room. There had been a time when he would have been afraid to wander through the empty school in the darkness, but the night no longer held any fear for him. And he knew the building with its twisting corridors and sudden, plunging staircases so well that he didn't even need to carry a torch.

With the wooden stairs creaking beneath his feet, he made his way to the ground floor. Which door had he heard open and close? Ahead of him, the main entrance to the school rose up about ten metres, a great wall of oak studded with iron. The door was bolted securely from inside so Vincent couldn't have passed through there. Behind him, going back underneath the staircase, a second door led into the Great Hall, where meals were served.

This door was open but the room behind it was shrouded in darkness and silent but for the flutter of the bats that lived high up in the rafters.

David reached the bottom of the staircase and stood silently on the cold, marble floor. He was surrounded by oil paintings, portraits of former heads and teachers; a true collection of old masters. All of them seemed to be looking at him, and as he moved forward the eyes swivelled to follow him and he heard a strange, musty whispering as the pictures muttered to one another.

"Where's he going? What's he doing?"

"He's making a mistake!"

"Don't do it, David."

"Go back to bed, David."

David ignored them. To one side a passage stretched out into the darkness, blocked at the end by a door he knew led into the library.

There were two more doors facing each other halfway along the passage. The one on the left led into the office of Mr Kilgraw, the assistant headmaster. As usual it was closed and no light showed through the crack. But on the other side of the passageway ... David felt the hairs on the back of his neck tingle. A square of light stretched out underneath the door. This one was marked HEADS. The room behind it belonged of course to Mr Fitch and Mr Teagle.

David was certain they weren't in their study. Only that afternoon they had complained of the very worst thing they could possibly get – a headache – and had announced they were going to bed early. Mr Fitch and Mr Teagle had no choice but to sleep in the same bed (though with two pillows) and rather curiously both men talked in their sleep, often having animated conversations right through the night.

But if Vincent was behind the door, what was he doing there? Going as quietly as he could – even the slightest movement seemed to echo throughout the school – David tiptoed along the corridor. Slowly, he reached out for the handle, his hand throwing an elongated shadow across the door. He hadn't even worked out what he would do when he discovered Vincent. But that didn't matter. He just wanted to see him.

He opened the door and blinked. The room was empty.

Closing the door behind him, David entered the heads' inner sanctum. The room was more like a chapel than a study, with its black marble floor and stained-glass windows. The furniture was solid and heavy, the desk a great block of wood that could have been an altar. Leather-bound books lined the walls, the shelves sagging under their weight. David knew he would be in serious trouble if he was found here. Nobody was allowed in this room unless summoned. But it was too late to turn back now.

The light that he had seen came from a lamp on a chest of drawers that stretched the whole length of the room. David ran his eyes along the surface, past a tangle of test-tubes and pipes, a stuffed rat, a human skull, a laptop, a pair of thumbscrews and a German helmet from the First World War. He was puzzled. What, he wondered, was the laptop for?

But this was no time to ask questions. Vincent wasn't in the room. That was all that mattered. *He* shouldn't be here either. He had to go.

It was as he turned to leave that he saw it. There was a small table in the far corner with a circular hole in the wall just above it. A picture lay face up on the carpet nearby. A safe! Somebody had taken down the picture and opened the safe. Like a moth to a flame he moved towards the table. There were four sheets of paper lying on the top. David knew what they were even before he reached out and picked them up. He looked down at the front cover.

GROOSHAM GRANGE EXAMINING BOARD
General Certificate of Secondary Education
ADVANCED CURSING

He was standing beside the open safe, holding the exam papers when the door crashed open behind him. With a dreadful lurching feeling in his stomach he looked round, knowing that he had been set up, knowing that it was too late to do anything about it. Mr Fitch and Mr Teagle were there, wearing dressing-gown and pyjamas. With them (and this was the only surprise) was Mr Helliwell. He was fully dressed. All three men – or all two and a half – were gazing at him in disbelief.

"David...!" Mr Fitch exclaimed. His long, hooked nose curved towards David accusingly.

"What are you doing here?" Mr Teagle demanded. He was wearing a nightcap with a pompom dangling just next to his chin. He shook his head disapprovingly and the pompom swung back and forth as if in agreement.

"I never thought it would be you, David," Mr

200

Helliwell said. The voodoo teacher looked genuinely astonished – and sad. He turned to the heads. "I heard someone go into your office," he explained. "But I never dreamed…"

"You were quite right to come to us, Mr Helliwell," Mr Fitch said.

"Quite right," Mr Teagle agreed.

"You can leave us now," Mr Fitch continued. "We'll take care of this."

Mr Helliwell paused as if he was about to say something. He glanced at David and shook his head. Then, with a quiet "Good night", he turned and left the room.

Mr Fitch and Mr Teagle remained where they were.

"Do you have anything to say for yourself, David?" Mr Teagle asked.

David thought for a moment. The bitterness of his defeat was in his mouth and he wanted to spit it out. But he knew when he was beaten. Somehow he had been lured into a trap. The portraits had tried to warn him but he hadn't listened and now it was too late to talk himself out of it. What could he say? The safe was open. The exam papers were in his hand. There was nobody else in the room. Trying to explain would only make matters worse.

He shook his head.

"Really, I am very disappointed in you," Mr Fitch said.

"And I am disappointed too," Mr Teagle stroked his beard. "It's not just that you were cheating. That would be bad enough."

"But you were *caught* cheating," Mr Fitch continued. "That's even worse. How could you be so clumsy? So amateurish?"

"And why did you even bother?" Mr Teagle asked. "You would easily have come first in Advanced Cursing without stealing the papers. Now we'll have to change all the questions. Completely rewrite the exam..."

"The exam is on Wednesday," Mr Fitch sighed. "That only gives us two days."

"We have no choice," Mr Teagle said. "We'll have to start again." He turned to David. "You won't believe this," he went on, "but writing exams is almost as boring as doing them! It's all most annoying."

Both men nodded at the same time, narrowly missing banging their heads together. Still David said nothing. He was furious with himself. He had walked into this. How could he have been so stupid?

"Are you aware of the seriousness of this offence?" Mr Teagle asked.

David was blushing darkly. He couldn't keep silent any longer. "It's not the way it looks," he said. "It's not what you think…"

"Oh no," Mr Fitch interrupted. "I suppose you're going to tell us that you were framed."

"Maybe you didn't mean to come in here and look at the exams," Mr Teagle suggested, sarcastically.

David hung his head low. "No," he whispered.

"Do you realize the gravity of this offence?" Mr Fitch asked.

"Very grave," Mr Teagle agreed. "Very grave indeed."

Mr Fitch sighed. "Sometimes I wonder, David, if you're suited to Groosham Grange. When you first came here, you fought against us. In a way you're still fighting. Do you really think you belong here?"

Did he belong at Groosham Grange? It was something that, in his darker moments, he had often wondered.

When he had first come to the school, he had indeed fought against it. As soon as he had learned about the secret lessons in black magic he had done everything he could to escape, to tell the authorities what he knew, to get the place closed down. It had only been when he had found himself trapped and helpless that he had changed his mind. If you can't beat them…

But here he was, a year later, determined to become the number one student, to win the

Unholy Grail. He remembered the fear he had once felt, the sense of horror. Classes in black magic! Ghosts and vampires! Now he was one of them – so what exactly did that make him? What had he become in the year he had been here?

He became aware of the heads, waiting for an answer.

"I do belong here," he said. "I know that now. But..." He hesitated. "I'm not evil."

"Evil?" Mr Teagle smiled for the first time. "What is good and what is evil?" he asked. "Sometimes it's not as easy as you think to tell them apart. That's still something you have to learn."

David nodded. "Maybe that's true," he said. "But all I know is ... this is my home. And I do want to stay."

"That's good. I'm glad to hear it." Mr Fitch was suddenly business-like. "But tonight's performance is going to cost you ten marks..."

"Fifteen," Mr Teagle cut in.

"...fifteen marks. Do you have anything to say?"

David shook his head. He was feeling sick to the stomach. Fifteen marks! Add that to the twelve marks he had lost earlier in the day and that left...

"David?"

...just three marks. Three marks between

Vincent and him. How had it happened? How had Vincent managed to lure him here?

"No, sir." His voice was hoarse, a whisper.

"Then I suggest you go back to bed."

"Yes..."

David was still holding the exam papers. Clenching his teeth, feeling the bitterness rising inside him, he jerked his fingers open, dropping them back on to the table. He hadn't read a single question.

He left the study and walked back along the passage and past the portraits, trying to ignore them tut-tutting at him as he went. With his mind still spinning, he climbed the stairs and found his way back to the dormitory. He stopped by his bed. Vincent was back. His clothes were on the chair, his body curled up under the blankets as if he had never been away. But was he really asleep? David gazed through the darkness at the half smile on the other boy's face and doubted it.

Silently, David undressed again and got back into bed. Three marks. That was all there was between them. Over and over again he muttered the figure to himself until at last he fell into an angry, restless sleep.

THE EXAM

Wednesday quickly came and with it the last examination of the year: Advanced Cursing.

There was a tradition at Groosham Grange that all the ordinary exams were taken upstairs, in the Great Hall. But for the more secretive ones, the exams relating to witchcraft and black magic, the pupils went downstairs through the network of tunnels and secret passages that lay beneath the school and into an underground chamber where sixty-five desks and sixty-five chairs had been set up, far away from the prying sun. This, then, was to be the final testing ground: a hidden cavern amongst the stalactites and stalagmites with a great waterfall of crystallized rock guarding the way out.

The exam was to start at eleven o'clock. At a quarter to, David made his way downstairs. His mouth was dry and he had an unpleasant feeling in the pit of his stomach. It was crazy. When it came to Advanced Cursing, everyone agreed he was untouchable. At the same time, he knew that it was one of Vincent's weakest subjects. That morning he had checked the league table one last time. He was still in first place. Vincent was three marks behind. After that there was a gap of seventeen marks to Jill, who was in third place. Looking at the notice-board had told him what he wanted to know. This exam was between him and Vincent. And Vincent didn't have a chance.

So why was he feeling so nervous? David opened the door of the library and went in. Ahead of him there was a full-length mirror and he glanced at his reflection while he walked towards it. He was tired and it showed. He hadn't slept well since his encounter in the heads' study. He was still having the dreams: his parents, the school breaking up and the face that he was sure he recognized.

He was right up against his reflection now. He scowled at himself briefly, then walked into the glass. The mirror rippled around him like water and then he had passed through it and into the first of the underground passages. His breath steamed slightly in the cold air as he followed the path down and he could feel the moisture clinging to his clothes. The examination room lay straight ahead, but on an impulse David took a fork, following a second passageway to the right. This was no more than a fissure in the rock, so narrow in places that he had to hold his breath to squeeze through. But then it widened out again and David found himself face to face with what he had come to see.

The Unholy Grail was kept in a miniature grotto, separated from the passageway by six iron bars. The bars were embedded in the rock, and there was no visible way through to the chamber behind. The Grail stood on a rock pedestal, bathed in an unnatural silver light. It was about fifteen centimetres high, a metallic grey in colour, encrusted with dark red stones that were either rubies or carbuncles. There was nothing very extraordinary about it to look at. But David found that his breath had caught in his throat. He was hypnotized by it. He could sense the power that the Grail contained and he would have given anything to reach through the bars and hold it in his hand.

This was what he was fighting for. He would take the exam and he would come first. Nobody would stop him.

"David...?"

Hearing his name, David swung round guiltily. He had been so absorbed in the Grail that he hadn't heard anyone approach. He turned and saw the arts, crafts and voodoo master, Mr Helliwell, standing at the entrance. He was wearing a dark, three-piece suit. It was the old-fashioned sort and made him look like a funeral director. "What are you doing here?" he asked.

"I was just looking..." David was being defensive. After their meeting two nights before, he had nothing more to say. But to his surprise Mr Helliwell moved closer and there was a frown of puzzlement on his face. "David," he began. "I want to talk to you about the other night."

"What about it?" David knew he was being deliberately rude but he was still angry about what had happened.

Mr Helliwell sighed. The light was reflecting off the huge dome of his head and his round, grey eyes seemed troubled. "I know you're upset," he said. "But there's something I have to tell you. I don't believe it was you who opened the safe."

"What?" David felt a surge of excitement.

"I was as surprised as anyone to find you in that room," the teacher went on. "Let me explain. I was doing my rounds when I saw someone come down the stairs. It was dark, so I didn't see who it was. But I could have sworn they had fair hair, lighter than yours."

Fair hair. That was Vincent. It had to be.

"I saw them go into the heads' study, and that was when I went to fetch Mr Fitch and Mr Teagle." Mr Helliwell paused. "Whoever was inside the study had left the door half open. I'd swear to that. Only, when we got back the door was closed. And *you* were inside."

"I didn't open the safe," David said. Now that he had started he couldn't stop. "Someone set me up. They wanted me to be found there. They knew you'd gone for the heads. And they must have slipped out just before I arrived."

"Someone...?" Mr Helliwell frowned. "Do you have any idea who?"

For a moment David was tempted to name Vincent King. But that wasn't the way he did things. He shook his head. "Why didn't you tell the heads what you'd seen?" he asked.

Mr Helliwell shrugged. "At the time it seemed an open and shut case. It was only afterwards..." He stroked his chin. "Even now I'm not sure. I suppose I believe you. But it's your word against..."

...against Vincent's. David nodded. The trap had been too well prepared.

Mr Helliwell pulled a fob-watch from his waistcoat pocket and looked at it. "It's almost eleven o'clock," he said. He reached out and put a firm, heavy hand on David's shoulder. "But if

210

you have any more problems, you come to me. Maybe I can help."

"Thank you." David turned and hurried back down the passageway. He was feeling ten times more confident than an hour before. He had let Vincent beat him once. There wouldn't be a second time.

He would take the exam and he would come first. And the Unholy Grail would be his.

* * *

GROOSHAM GRANGE EXAMINING BOARD
General Certificate of Secondary Education
ADVANCED CURSING
Wednesday 24 October 11.00 a.m.
TIME: 2 hours

Write your name and candidate number in ink (not in blood) on each side of the paper. Write on one side of the paper only, preferably not the thin side.

Answer *all* the questions. Each question is to be answered on a separate sheet.

The number of marks available is shown in brackets at the end of each question or part question. The total for this paper is 100 marks.

Candidates are warned not to attempt to curse the person who set this exam.

1. Write out in full the words of power that would cause the following curses (30):
    a) Baldness (5)
    b) Acne (5)
    c) Bad breath (5)
    d) Amnesia (5)
    e) Death (10)

CAUTION: Do not mutter the words of power as you write them. If anyone near you loses their hair, breaks out in spots, smells like an onion, forgets why they're here and/or dies, you will be disqualified.

2. Your aunt announces that she has come to stay for Christmas and New Year.

    She is seventy years old and leaves a lipstick mark on your cheek when she kisses you. Although you are fifteen, she still insists that you are nine. She criticizes your clothes, your hair and your taste in music. As usual, she has brought you a book token.

    Describe in two hundred words a suitable curse that would ensure she spends next Christmas in (10):

a) The intensive care unit of your local hospital OR
b) A rice field in China OR
c) A crater on the dark side of the moon

3. What is thanatomania? Define it, giving two historical examples. Then describe how you would survive it. (35)

4. Write down a suitable curse for THREE of the following people (15):
   a) Elephant poachers (5)
   b) People who talk in cinemas (5)
   c) Litter bugs (5)
   d) Cigarette manufacturers (5)
   e) Bullies (5)

5. Describe how you would re-create the Great Plague using ingredients found in your local supermarket. (10)

It was as easy as that.

As soon as David had run his eyes over the questions, he knew he was going to be all right. He had even revised the Great Plague a few nights before and the rest of the exam was just as straightforward.

So he was smiling when the clock struck one and Mr Helliwell called time. While everyone else remained in their seats, Vincent and another boy who had been sitting in the front row got up and started collecting the papers. It was Vincent who came over to David's desk. As he handed his answers over, David lifted his head and allowed his eyes to lock with Vincent's. He didn't say anything but he wanted the other boy to know. I got every question right. Nothing can stop me now.

Mr Helliwell dropped the papers into his leather bag and everyone was allowed to leave. Once they were back out in the open air, David caught up with Jill. It was a beautiful afternoon. The sun felt warm on his neck after the chill of the cave.

"How did it go?" he asked.

Jill grimaced. "Awful. What on earth is thinatomania?"

"Thanatomania. It's a sort of multiple curse," David explained. "It was when a witch wanted to hurt a whole town or village instead of just one person." He shuddered. "I don't know why they teach us about things like that. It's not as if we'd ever want to curse anyone."

"No," Jill agreed. "But most of the stuff you learn at school you never actually use. You just have to know about it, that's all." She took his arm. "So how did you do?"

David smiled. "It was easy."

"I'm glad you think so." Jill looked away. In

the distance, Vincent was walking off on his own towards the East Tower. He was smiling and there was a spring in his step. "I wouldn't count your chickens too soon," she said. "There goes Vincent. And he looks pretty confident too."

David remembered her words over the next few days. There were more lessons but with the final exam over, the league table was officially closed. Everything now hinged on Advanced Cursing and although David was sure of himself, although he pretended he wasn't thinking about it, he still found himself hanging around the notice-board near the heads' study where the results would eventually be posted.

And he was there one evening when Mr Kilgraw, the assistant headmaster, appeared, a sheet of paper in one hand and a drawing pin in the other. David felt his heartbeat quicken. There was a lump in his throat and a tingling in the palms of his hands. Nobody else was around. He would be the first to know the result.

Forcing himself not to run, he went over to the notice-board. Mr Kilgraw gave him a deathly smile. "Good evening, David."

"Good evening, sir." Why didn't Mr Kilgraw say anything? Why didn't he congratulate David on coming first, on winning the Unholy Grail?

With difficulty, he forced his eyes up to take in the notice-board. And there it was:

ADVANCED CURSING – RESULTS

But the name on the top was not his own.

Linda James, the girl who had been disintegrated by Mrs Windergast, was first.

David blinked. What about the name underneath her?

William Rufus had come second.

Then Jeffrey Joseph.

It wasn't possible.

"A very disappointing result for you, David." Mr Kilgraw was talking, but David hardly heard him. He was panicking now. The typed letters on the list were blurring into each other as he searched through them for his name. There was Vincent, in ninth place with sixty-eight points. And there he was, two places below … eleventh! He had scored only sixty-five. It was impossible!

"Very disappointing," Mr Kilgraw said, but there was something strange in his voice. It was as soft and as menacing as ever, but there was something else. Was he pleased?

Eleventh… David felt numb. He tried to work out where it left him on the league table. Linda had scored seventy-six points. He was eleven behind her, three behind Vincent. He had lost the Grail. He must have.

"I was quite surprised," Mr Kilgraw went on. "I would have thought you would have known the meaning of thanatomania."

"Thanato...?" David's voice seemed to be coming from a long way away. He turned to Mr Kilgraw. He could hear footsteps approaching. News had got out that the results were there. Soon there would be a crowd. "But I *do* know," David said. "I wrote it down..."

Mr Kilgraw shook his head with a sad smile. "I marked the papers myself," he said. "You didn't even tackle the question."

"But ... I did! I got it right!"

"No, David. It was Question Three. I must say, you got everything else right. But I'm afraid you lost thirty-five points on that one. You didn't hand in an answer."

Hand in an answer...

And then David remembered. Vincent had collected the papers. He had handed them to Vincent. And following the instructions at the top of the exam, each question had been answered on a separate sheet. It would have been simple for Vincent to slip one of the pages out. David had been so confident, so sure of himself, that he hadn't even thought of it. But that must have been what had happened. That was the only possibility.

There were about twenty or thirty people milling around the notice-board now, struggling to get closer, calling out names and numbers. David heard his own name called out. Eleventh with sixty-five points.

"That means he's first equal," somebody shouted. "He and Vincent King have tied in first place."

"So who gets the Unholy Grail?"

Everybody was chattering around him. Feeling sick and confused, David pushed his way through the crowd and ran off, ignoring Jill and the others who were calling after him.

There was no moon that night. As if to add to the darkness, a mist had rolled in from the sea, slithering over the damp earth and curling up against the walls of Groosham Grange. Everything was silent. Even Gregor – sound asleep on one of the tombstones in the cemetery – was actually making no sound. Normally he snored. Tonight he was still.

Nobody heard the door creak open to one side of the school. Nobody saw a figure step out into the night and make its way over the moss and the soil towards the East Tower. A second door opened and closed. Inside the tower, a light flickered on.

But nobody saw the lantern as it turned

round and round on itself, being carried ever higher up the spiral staircase that led to the battlements. A bloated spider scuttled out of the way, just managing to avoid the heel of a black leather shoe that pounded down on the concrete step. A rat arched its back in a corner, fearful of the unaccustomed light. But no human eye was open. No human ear heard the thud, thud, thud of footsteps climbing the stairs.

The secret agent reached a circular room at the top of the tower, its eight narrow windows open to the night. To one side there was a table, some paper and what looked like a collection of boxes. From inside the boxes came the sound of flapping and a strange, high-pitched squeak. The agent sat down and drew one of the sheets of paper forward. And began to write:

TOP SECRET
To the Bishop of Bletchley

All is going according to plan. Nobody suspects. Very soon the Unholy Grail will be ours. Expect further news soon.

Once again there was no signature at the bottom of the page. The agent scrawled a single X, then folded the letter carefully and reached into one of the boxes. It wasn't actually a box but a cage. His hand came out again holding something that looked like a scrap of torn leather except that it was alive, jerking and squealing. The agent attached the message to the creature's leg, then carried it over to the window.

"Off you go." The words were a soft whisper in the darkness.

A brief flurry. A last cry. And then the message was gone, carried off into the swirling night.

NEEDLE IN A
HAYSTACK

"It's a very unusual situation," Mr Fitch said. "We have a tie."

"David Eliot and Vincent King," Mr Teagle agreed. "Both have six hundred and sixty-six points."

"It's a bit of a beast," Mr Fitch remarked, tetchily. "What are we going to do?"

Both men – or rather, both heads – looked round the table. The two of them were in the staff room, sitting in a single, high-backed chair. It was midday. Arranged around the table in front of them were Mr Kilgraw, Mr Helliwell, Mr Creer, Mrs Windergast, Monsieur Leloup and the oldest teacher in the school (by several centuries), Miss Pedicure. Miss Pedicure taught English and history, although at the start of her career there hadn't been any history to teach (as nothing had happened) and English hadn't been invented.

People either spoke Norse or simply grunted. She was now so frail and wrinkled that everyone would stop and stare whenever she sneezed, afraid that the effort might cause her to disintegrate.

Mr Kilgraw grimaced, for a moment revealing two razor-sharp vampire teeth. There was a glass of red liquid on the table in front of him which might have been wine, but probably wasn't. "Is it not a tradition," he enquired, "in this circumstance to set some sort of trial? A tie-breaker?"

"What sort of trial do you have in mind?" Mrs Windergast asked.

Mr Kilgraw waved a languid hand. Because it was the middle of the day, the curtains in the room had been drawn for him but enough of the light was filtering through to make him even paler than usual. "It will have to take place off the island," he said. "I would suggest London."

"Why London?" Miss Pedicure demanded.

"London is the capital," Mr Kilgraw replied. "It is polluted, over-crowded and dangerous. A perfect arena..."

"Here, here!" Mrs Windergast muttered.

"You agree?" Mr Kilgraw asked.

"No. I was saying that the trial ought to take place here, here ... on the island."

"No," Mr Fitch rapped his knuckles on the table. "It's better if we send them out. More challenging."

"I have an idea," Mr Kilgraw said.

"Do tell us," Mr Fitch gurgled.

"Over the last year we have tested these boys in every aspect of the magical arts," Mr Kilgraw began. "Cursing, levitation, shape-changing, thanatomania…"

"What's thanatomania?" Mr Creer demanded.

Mr Kilgraw ignored him. "I suggest we set them a puzzle," he went on. "It will be a trial of skill and of the imagination. A meeting of two minds. It will take me a day or two to work out the details. But at least it will be final. Whoever wins the contest comes top of the league and takes the Unholy Grail."

Everyone around the table murmured their assent. Mr Fitch glanced at Mr Helliwell. "Does it seem fair to you, Mr Helliwell?" he asked.

The voodoo master nodded gravely. "I think that David Eliot deserves the Grail," he said. "If you ask me, there's something funny about the way he's lost so many marks in such a short time. But this will give him a chance to prove himself. I'm sure he'll win. So I agree."

"Then it's decided," Mr Teagle concluded. "Mr Kilgraw will work on the tie-breaker. And perhaps you'll let me know when you've sorted something out."

Two days later, David and Vincent stood in one

of the underground caverns of Skrull Island. They were both dressed casually in jeans and black, open-neck shirts. Mr Kilgraw, Mr Helliwell and Miss Pedicure were standing opposite them. At the back of the cave were two glass boxes that could have been shower cubicles except that they were empty. The boxes looked slightly ridiculous in the gloomy setting of the cave – like two theatrical props that had wandered off stage. But David knew what they were. One was for Vincent. The other was for him.

"You are to look for a needle in a haystack," Mr Kilgraw was saying. "Some needles are bigger than others – and that may point you in the right direction. But the needle in question is a small statue of Miss Pedicure. I will tell you only that it is blue in colour and six centimetres high."

"It was taken from my mummy some years ago," Miss Pedicure sniffed. "I've always wanted to have it back."

"As for the haystack," Mr Kilgraw went on, "that is the British Museum in London. All I will tell you is that the statue is somewhere inside. You have until midnight to find it. And there is one rule…" He nodded at Mr Helliwell.

"You are not to use any magical powers," the voodoo teacher said. "We want this to be a test of stealth and cunning. We have helped you boys a little. We have arranged for the alarm system at the museum to turn itself off tonight and we have opened one door. But there will still be guards on duty. If you're caught, that's your own problem."

"It's seven o'clock now," Mr Kilgraw said. "You have just five hours. Do you both understand what you have to do?"

David and Vincent nodded.

"Then let us begin. Whichever of you finds the statuette first and brings it back to this room will be declared the winner and will be awarded the Unholy Grail."

David glanced at Vincent. The two of them hadn't spoken to each other since the results of the exam had been announced. The tension between them almost crackled like static electricity. Vincent swept a blond lock of hair off his face. "I'll be waiting for you when you get back," he said.

"I'll be back here first," David replied.

They stepped into the boxes.

"Let the tie-breaker begin," Mr Kilgraw commanded.

David felt the air inside the box go suddenly cold. He had been standing with his hands pressed against the glass, looking at Mr Kilgraw. Then, slowly at first but accelerating quickly, the glass box began to turn. It was like a fairground ride except that there was no music, no sound at all, and he didn't feel sick or giddy. Mr Kilgraw spun past him, a blur of colour that had lost all sense of shape, blending in with the walls of the cave as the box turned faster and faster. Now the whole world had dissolved into a wheel of silver and grey. Then the lights went out.

David closed his eyes. When he opened them a moment later, he found he was looking at a street and a hedge. Swallowing, he pulled his hands away from the glass, leaving two damp palm prints behind. The box was illuminated from above by a single, yellow bulb. A car drove past along the street, its headlights on. David twisted round. Something bumped against his shoulder.

He was in a telephone box. Not a modern kiosk but one of the old, red telephone boxes with a swinging door that stood in the middle of Regent's Park, London. It took him a moment to open it but then he was standing on the pavement, breathing the night air. There was no sign of Vincent. He looked at his watch. Seven o'clock. He had travelled two hundred kilometres in less than a second.

But he was still a long way from the museum. Vincent would already be on his way. And this was his last chance...

David crossed the road and broke into a run.

In fact he took a taxi to the museum. He caught one in Baker Street and ordered the driver to go as fast as possible.

"The British Museum? You must be joking, mate! There's no point going there now. It's closed for the night. Anyway, aren't you a bit young to be out on your own? You got any money?"

David had no money. Neither of the boys had been given any – it was part of the test. Quickly, he hypnotized the driver. He knew he wasn't allowed to use magic, but Mr Kilgraw had often told him that hypnosis was a science and not a magical power, so he decided it wouldn't count.

"The British Museum," he insisted. "And put your foot down."

"Foot down? All right, guv'nor. Whatever you say. You're the boss." The driver shot through a red light, zigzagged across a busy intersection with cars hooting at him on all sides and accelerated the wrong way down a one-way street. The journey took them about ten minutes and David was relieved to get out.

He paid the driver with a leaf and two pebbles he had picked up in the park. "Keep the change," he said.

"Cor! Thanks, guv'nor." The cab driver's eyes

were still spinning. David watched him as he drove off across a pavement and into a shop window, then slipped through the open gates of the British Museum.

But why were the gates open?

Had Mr Helliwell arranged it for him? Or had Vincent got there first?

Feeling very small and vulnerable, David crossed the open space in front of the museum. The building itself was huge, bigger than he remembered. He had once heard that there were four kilometres of galleries inside and looking at it now, its classical pillars arranged in two wings around a vast, central chamber, he could well believe it. His feet clattered faintly across the concrete as he ran forward. A well-cut lawn, grey in the moonlight, stretched out as flat as paper on either side of him. There was a guard-hut next to the gate but it was deserted. His shadow raced ahead of him, snaking up the steps as if trying to get into the building before him.

The main entrance to the museum was locked. For a moment David was tempted. A single spell would open the door. He could simply move the tumblers inside the lock with the power of thought or else he could turn himself into smoke and creep in through the crack underneath. But Mr Helliwell had said:

no magic. And this time David was determined not to cheat. He would play by the rules.

It took him ten minutes to locate the side door that Mr Kilgraw had opened. He slipped through and found himself standing on a stone floor beneath a ceiling that was so far above him that, in the half light, he could barely see it. Doors led off to the left and right. Straight ahead there was an information desk and what looked like a souvenir shop. A grand staircase guarded by two stone lions swept up to one side. Which way should he go?

It was only now that he was here that David grasped the enormity of the task that faced him. Miss Pedicure had lived for three thousand years. And she had lived in just about every part of the world. So this statue of her – which had once belonged to her mother – could come from anywhere and any time. It was six centimetres high and it was blue. That was all he knew.

So much for the needle. But what of the haystack?

The British Museum was enormous. How many exhibits did it hold? Ten thousand? A hundred thousand? Some of them were the size of small buildings. Some of them, in fact, *were* small buildings. Others were no bigger than a pin. The museum held collections from Ancient Greece, Ancient Egypt, Babylon, Persia, China; from the

Iron Age, the Bronze Age, the Middle Ages, every age. There were tools and pottery, clocks and jewellery, masks and ivory... He could spend a year in the place and still get nowhere close.

David heard the rattle of a chain and pressed himself back against the wall, well into the shadows. A guard appeared, walking down the stairs and into the main hall. He was dressed in blue trousers and a white shirt, with a bunch of keys dangling from his waist. He paused in the middle of the entrance hall, yawned and stretched his arms, then disappeared behind the information desk.

Crouching in the dark, David considered. As far as he could see, he had two choices. One: search the museum as quickly as he could and hope he would strike lucky. Two: look for some sort of catalogue and try to find the statuette listed there. But even if a catalogue existed, how would he know what to look for? It was hardly likely that Miss Pedicure's name would turn up in the index and there were probably statuettes in just about every room in the building.

That only left the first option. Straightening up again, David crossed the hall and climbed the staircase that the guard had just come down. He would have to hope for a little luck.

Three and a half hours later he was back where he'd started.

His head was pounding and his eyes were sore with fatigue. The stairs had led him up past a Roman mosaic and on into Medieval Britain. He had back-tracked into the Early Bronze Age (dodging a second guard) and had somehow found his way into Ancient Syria ... which was indeed seriously ancient. He must have looked at about ten thousand objects all neatly laid out in their glass cases. He felt like a window-shopper in some sort of insane supermarket and he hadn't found anything remotely like Miss Pedicure's statuette. After a while, he barely knew what he was looking at. Whether it was a Late Babylonian jug or an Early Sumerian mug no longer made any difference to him. David had never been very fond of museums. But this was torture.

Standing once again in the entrance hall, he looked at his watch. It was a quarter to eleven. Less than two hours of the challenge remained ... assuming that Vincent hadn't found the statuette and left with it long ago.

Another guard crossed the entrance hall. "Who's there?" he called out.

David froze. He couldn't be found, not now. But then a second guard, a woman, appeared from the door on the right. "It's only me."

"Wendy? I thought I heard someone..."

"Yeah. This place gives me the shivers. I've

been hearing things all night. Footsteps..."

"Me too. Fancy a cup of tea?"

"Yeah. I'll put the kettle on..."

The two guards walked off together and David ducked back through another open door just opposite the main entrance. It led into the most amazing room he had ever seen.

It was vast, stretching the entire length of the museum. It was filled with a bizarre collection of animals, people, and creatures that were both. Everything looked Egyptian. Huge Pharaohs carved in black stone sat with their hands on their knees, frozen solid as they had been for thousands of years. On one side, two bearded men with lions' feet and dragons' wings crouched, staring at each other in grim silence. On the other, a gigantic tiger stood poised as if about to leap into the darkness. Further down the gallery there were animals of all shapes and sizes, facing in different directions like guests at a nightmare cocktail party.

David froze. He had seen Vincent before he had heard him. The other boy was moving incredibly quietly and would himself have seen David had he not been looking the other way. David noticed that Vincent had taken his shoes off and was holding them in his hand. It was a good idea and one that David should have thought of himself.

Vincent was looking as lost and as tired as David. Crouching down behind a brass baboon, David watched him pass. As he went, Vincent rubbed his forehead with the back of one hand and David almost felt sorry for him. He had never liked Vincent and he didn't trust him. But he knew what he was going through now.

A minute later Vincent had gone. David stood up. Which way now? Vincent hadn't found the statue yet, and that was good, but it didn't help him. He looked once more at his watch. There was little over an hour left.

Left or right? Up or down?

At the far end of the gallery he could see a collection of sarcophagi and several obelisks – some carved with hieroglyphics like Cleopatra's Needle – plus four gods with the heads of cats.

And that was when he knew.

In fact he should have known from the start. This challenge was all about skill, not chance. Mr Helliwell had said it himself: *a test of stealth and cunning*. What he and Mr Kilgraw had said, what Miss Pedicure had said, and what he had just seen ... put them all together and the answer was obvious.

David knew where he was going now. He should have known hours ago. He looked around him for a sign, then ran off down the gallery.

He just hoped he wasn't already too late.

WAX

Between them, Mr Kilgraw, Mr Helliwell and Miss Pedicure had given him all the clues he could have asked for. David played back what they had said.

Some needles are bigger than others ... that may point you in the right direction.

Well, David had just seen the biggest needle of all – a stone pillar that had made him think of Cleopatra's Needle on the Thames. And what direction had that come from? Egypt!

And then Miss Pedicure: *It was taken from my mummy...*

She wasn't talking about her mother, of course. The statuette had been buried with her, part of an Egyptian mummy.

That was where he was going now. The head of a giant ram watched him without interest as he plunged into the Egyptian rooms of the museum. The statuette would be somewhere here – he was certain. How could he have wasted so much time? If only he'd stopped and thought first...

The first room he entered was filled with more sarcophagi – the stone coffins that contained the mummies. There were about a dozen of them on display, brightly coloured and strangely cheerful. It was as if the Ancient Egyptians had chosen to gift-wrap their dead. Some of the cases were open and, glancing inside, David saw hunched, shrivelled-up figures in dirty grey bandages. Strange to think that Miss Pedicure had once looked like that – although when it was raining and she was in a bad mood, she sometimes still did.

David hurried into the next room. What he was looking for would be displayed separately, in one of the side cases. How much time did he have left? There were still hundreds of objects on display all around him. His eyes raced past dolls, toys, mummified cats and snakes, jugs, cups, jewellery ... and then he had found it! It was right in front of him, a blue figure about the size of his hand, lying on its back as if sunbathing. David rested his hand on the glass and stared at the little doll, at its black hair, thin face and tapered waist. He recognized Miss Pedicure at once. The statue was labelled:

Glazed Companion doll. XVIIIth Dynasty. 1450 BC.

It was incredible. The English and history teacher had hardly changed in three thousand years. She was even carrying the same handbag.

Somebody coughed at the end of the gallery and David froze. But it was only another guard, making for a side room and an early-twenty-first century cup of tea. He tilted his watch. It was just after eleven. He had more time than he thought. He lifted the cover of the glass case and took out the statuette.

The Unholy Grail was his.

At half past eleven, David climbed the escalator at Baker Street tube station and emerged into the street. He had preferred to take the train back to Regent's Park, losing himself in the crowds underground. It was only a ten-minute walk back to the telephone box. The statuette was safely in his pocket. He had plenty of time.

It was a cool evening with a touch of drizzle in the breeze. David wondered where Vincent might be now. The other boy was probably still in the British Museum, desperately searching for the statue. Even if he did work out the puzzle and find the display case, he was too late. It was too bad. But the best man had won.

A motorcyclist accelerated through a puddle,

sending the water in a spray that just missed David. On the other side of the road, a bus without passengers rumbled through a yellow light and turned towards the West End. David continued on past Madame Tussaud's. His father had taken him to the famous waxworks museum once but it hadn't been a successful trip. "Not enough bankers!" Mr Eliot had exclaimed and had left without even visiting the Chamber of Horrors. The long, windowless building was silent. The pavement outside, crowded with tourists and ice-cream sellers by day, was empty, glistening under the street lights.

David felt a gust of cold air tug at the collar of his shirt. Behind him he heard the sound of splintering wood. He thought nothing of it. But unconsciously he quickened his pace.

The road continued up to a set of traffic lights. This was where Regent's Park began – David could see it in the distance, a seemingly endless black space. He glanced behind him. Although the pavement had been empty before, there was now a single figure, staggering about as if drunk. It was a man, wearing some sort of uniform and boots. He was weaving small circles on the pavement, his arms outstretched, his feet jerking into the air. It was as if he had never walked before, as if he were trying to find his balance.

David turned the corner, leaving the drunk – if that was what he was – behind. He was beginning to feel uneasy but he still didn't know why.

The path he was following crossed a main road and then continued over a humpback bridge. Suddenly he was out of the hubbub of London. The darkness and emptiness of Regent's Park was all around him, enclosing him in its ancient arms. Somewhere a dog barked in the night.

"Just slow down…"

He muttered the words to himself, somehow relieved to hear the sound of his own voice. Once again he looked at his watch. A quarter to twelve. Plenty of time. How had he allowed one crazy drunk to spook him like this? Smiling, he looked back over his shoulder.

The smile died on his lips.

The man had followed him into the park. He was standing on the bridge now, lit by a lamp directly above him. In the last few minutes he had learnt how to walk properly and he was standing to attention, his eyes glittering in the light. He was much closer and David could see him clearly – the brown boots, the belt, the strap running across his chest. He wasn't wearing a uniform but a sort of brown suit, the trousers ballooning out at the thighs. David recognized him instantly. He would have known even without the black swastika in the red and white armband on the man's right arm. How could he fail to recognize the thin black hair sweeping down over the pale face and, of course, the famous moustache?

Adolf Hitler!

Or at least, Adolf Hitler's waxwork.

David remembered the gust of cold air he had felt. There was always a touch of coldness in the air when black magic was being performed and the blacker the spell the more intense the coldness. He had felt it but he had ignored it. And the splintering sound! The creature must have broken the door to get out. Who could have animated it? Vincent? David stared at the Hitler waxwork, feeling sick. And even as he backed away, a horrible thought occurred to him. Hitler had been first out of Madame Tussaud's. But was he alone?

The question was answered a second later. The Hitler waxwork jerked forward, his legs jackknifing in the air. Behind him, two more figures appeared, rising like zombies over the top of the humpback bridge. David didn't wait to see who they might be. Three words were echoing in his mind.

Chamber of Horrors.

He tried to remember who was exhibited in that part of Madame Tussaud's. He had a nasty feeling he might be meeting them at any moment.

David turned and ran. But it was only now that he saw how carefully the trap had been laid. Three more waxworks had made their way into the park and were approaching him from the other direction. One was dressed only in a dirty white night-gown and black clogs. It was carrying something in its hands. David stared. It was a victim of the French Revolution. It was carrying its head! Behind it came two short men in prison uniform. David didn't recognize either of them – but they had recognized him. Their eyes seemed to light up as they shuffled forward, arms outstretched. David saw a gate in the fence, half open. He ran through it and into the inner heart of the park.

He found himself on a patch of lawn with a set of tennis courts to one side and an unpleasant, stagnant pool on the other. The field was dotted with trees and he made for the nearest one, grateful at least that it was a dark night. But even as he ran, the clouds parted and a huge moon broke through like a searchlight. Was that part of the magic too? Was Vincent even controlling the weather?

In the white, ghostly light, the whole park had changed. It was like something out of a bad dream. Everything was black, white and grey.

The Hitler waxwork had already reached the gate and passed through with the two prisoners. The French Revolution victim had been left behind. This waxwork had tripped over a tree root and lost its head and although the head was shouting "Over here!" the rest of the body hadn't found it yet.

But that was the only good news.

Another half dozen waxworks had somehow found their way to the park and were spreading out, searching through the trees. There was a man dressed entirely in black with a doctor's bag in one hand and a huge, curving knife in the other. Jack the Ripper! And right behind him came a lady in Victorian dress, horribly stabbed, blood (wax blood, David had to remind himself) pouring out of a gaping wound in her chest. She had to be one of the women he had killed. Behind him, David heard a dreadful gurgling sound and turned just in time to see a third, white-faced waxwork rising through the scummy surface of the pool. The models were everywhere. David crouched behind a tree, trying to lose himself in it. He was surrounded and knew that it was only a matter of time before he was found.

"There he is, Adolf!" somebody shouted.

A short, dark-haired man in a double-breasted suit had climbed out of a ditch, an ugly scar twisting down his wax cheek. It was a face that David recognized from old black and white films: the American gangster, Al Capone. He walked quickly across the grass, then brought his hands up in front of his chest. There was a metallic click. Capone was holding a machine-gun. He had just loaded it.

With his breath rasping in his throat, David left the cover of the tree and broke into a run. The wax models were all around him, some like sleepwalkers, others more like clockwork toys as they scuttled forward. He felt horribly exposed out in the moonlight but he had no choice. He had to find the telephone box, but where was it? He made a quick calculation and started forward, then dived to the ground as a spray of machine-gun bullets sliced through the air, a centimetre above his head. Al Capone had fired at him. And somehow David knew that the bullets were the one thing there that weren't made of wax.

Someone stepped out in front of him, blocking his way. It was a small man in an old-fashioned wing-collar shirt and a smart grey suit. He had wispy, ginger hair and a small moustache. His eyes twinkled behind round, wire-framed glasses. The man held up the palms of his hands. "It's all right," he said. "I'm a doctor."

"A doctor?" David panted.

"Yes. Doctor Crippen!"

The man had pulled out a vicious-looking hypodermic syringe. David yelled and lashed out with his fist, catching the little man straight on the nose. He felt his fist sink into the soft wax and when he jerked it back he had left a round imprint inside the figure's head. David ran. Behind him he could hear Hitler shouting out orders in manic German. Jack the Ripper was lumbering up behind him with the hideous knife raised above his head.

Meanwhile, another man, this one in gleaming silver armour, had just come in through the open gate. He had long black hair, tied behind his neck, and two of the cruellest eyes David had ever seen. Swords and daggers, at least a dozen of them, protruded from him in every direction. It was Attila the Hun, one of the most bloodthirsty warriors in history, and David had no doubt whose blood he was thirsting for now.

The grass curved round behind the tennis courts, bordered on the edge by a thicket of trees and shrubs. David plunged into the shadows, glad to be out of the glare of the moon. The darkness seemed to confuse the waxworks because they hung back, one or two of them bumping into each other, almost as if they were afraid to cross the line from light into dark. There was an iron fence straight ahead of him.

David ran over to it, grabbing it with both hands.

His heart was thudding madly in his chest and he stopped to catch his breath and give himself time to think. They hadn't got him yet! There was still time to reach the telephone box and make his way back to Groosham Grange. David jerked one hand down to his trouser pocket. The statuette was still there.

Vincent! He breathed the name through clenched teeth. This had to be Vincent's work. He must somehow have followed David from the museum and conjured up the spell as he walked past Madame Tussaud's. Of course, he had cheated. Vincent had broken the single rule of the contest – not to use magic – and the worst of it was that there was nothing David could do. What spell could he use to destroy the waxworks? And if he used magic, wouldn't he be disqualifying himself?

David was gripping the fence so hard that the metal bit into his hands. He looked over the top, into the next enclosure and for the first time since he had reached the park he felt a surge of hope. The telephone box was in sight – and it was unguarded. It was only ten to twelve. All he had to do was climb the fence and he would be home and dry!

He took one last look back. With Hitler at the

head of them, just about all the waxworks were congregating on the fence, a semicircle that had already begun to close in. Only two of the wax-works had stayed behind: the drowned man and the Victorian woman. They had found the Frenchman's lost head and, despite his protests, were playing tennis with it on one of the courts. Jack the Ripper was edging forward with a dia-bolical smile, his wax lips parted to reveal two jagged lines of wax teeth. Dr Crippen had two more syringes and a surgical knife. Al Capone was behind him, trying to elbow his way past. David wasn't sure if their glass eyes could make him out in the shadows. But slowly they were heading towards him.

It was time to go. He swung round, preparing to heave himself over the fence. Too late. He saw a movement out of the corner of his eye. Something hit him full in the face and he was thrown back, off his feet. For a moment the world spun and then his shoulders hit the earth and all his breath was punched out of him.

"It's all right, everyone! I've got him! Do come quickly!"

The voice was shrill and excited. There was a rustle of leaves and a snapping of twigs and a large woman dressed in blue stepped forward. David tried to stand but all his strength had left him. The woman was wearing a billowing velvet and silk dress that made her look enormous. Her head was crowned by a silver and diamond tiara that sparkled even out of the moonlight and there was a Weight Watchers badge pinned to her lapel. She hadn't come out of the Chamber of Horrors. Lying, dazed, on a bed of leaves, David instantly recognized the ginger hair and perfect smile of the Duchess of York. She had hit him with her handbag.

"Good work, Your Highness," Dr Crippen muttered. His wax nose was bent out of shape where David had hit him and one of his eyes had fallen out.

"Ja. Sehr gut, Fräulein Fergie," Hitler agreed.

David wrenched the statuette out of his pocket and tried to stand up. The park was spinning round him, moving faster and faster. He tried to speak, to utter a few words of some spell that might yet save him. But his mouth was dry and the words would not come. He looked up into the leering, lifeless faces that surrounded him and raised a hand. Then the Duchess hit him again and he was out cold.

THE EAST TOWER

"He's lying," David said. "I found the statuette. He stole it. And he used magic to do it."

David was standing in Mr Kilgraw's study with Vincent only a few paces away. His clothes were dishevelled and there was a large bruise above his cheek where the handbag had hit him. Mr Helliwell stood in one corner of the room, resting his chin on one hand, watching the two boys quietly. Mr Kilgraw sat behind his desk with the statuette in front of him. David felt like snapping it in half. And he felt much the same about Vincent.

"I admit he found it first," Vincent said. He took his hands out of his pockets. "I've told you. I worked out the puzzle and found the cabinet, but I was too late. I guessed David had taken it so I went back to the telephone box. That was when I saw him with the statuette lying next to him. I figured he must have tripped over or something so I took the statuette. I didn't see any waxworks though," he added.

"Didn't see them?" David curled his fists. "You sent them!"

"I had nothing to do with it."

"Then who did?"

"That's enough of this!" Mr Kilgraw said, fluttering his hand for silence. His voice was little more than a whisper, but then the assistant headmaster rarely spoke loudly. He leaned back in his chair. "The trial is over," he said. "And Vincent has won."

"But sir..." David began.

"No!" Mr Kilgraw pointed a finger. "David, you talk about cheating, but it seems to me that it was only a few days ago that you were discovered trying to steal the papers for the last exam."

"That was Vincent too," David replied. "He set me up."

"And then there's the question of Sports Day. The obstacle race..."

David fell silent. He was blushing and he knew it. The obstacle race! Mr Kilgraw had known about it all the time. There was nothing David could say now. He had cheated once in his life and because of that nobody would ever trust him again.

"We don't need to prolong this discussion," Mr Kilgraw said. "Whatever happened tonight, Vincent won. He was the first back and he brought the statue with him. Mr Helliwell...?"

In the corner, the voodoo teacher shrugged. "I'm sorry, David," he said. "But I have to agree."

"Then that's that. Vincent King takes first place on the league. At prize-giving it will be he who is presented with the Unholy Grail."

"Thank you, sir." Vincent glanced again at David. "I mean it, David," he said. "I didn't want it to happen this way."

"Like hell..."

"Don't ever compare anything to hell until you've been there!" Mr Kilgraw snapped, and now he was really angry. "I have to say you've been a complete disappointment, David. And not just tonight. Fighting in the corridor. Trying to steal the exam paper and then whining and complaining when you failed to answer all the questions. You used to be our most promising pupil. But now I even wonder if it's worth your staying here at Groosham Grange."

"So do I," David growled. He regretted the words as soon as they were out but it was too late. Mr Kilgraw had heard.

"That's a decision you have to make," he

said. "If you want to leave, nobody will stop you. But remember, once you've gone, you can't come back. We'll never see you again…"

David opened his mouth to speak but there was nothing to say. He took one last look at Vincent who was doing his best to avoid his eyes. Mr Helliwell sighed and shook his head. Mr Kilgraw's hand closed round the statue. "And now if you'll excuse me," he said, "this has to go back to the museum. It'll be daylight soon and we wouldn't want it to be missed."

Jill Green was waiting for David outside the study. She was about to ask him what had happened, but one look at his face told her all she needed to know.

"So he won then," she said.

David nodded.

"Does it really matter, David? I mean, what's so important about the Unholy Grail anyway?" She took his arm. "You're still the best magician in the school. You don't need a cup to prove it."

"I told Mr Kilgraw I wanted to leave Groosham Grange," David said.

"What?" Jill stiffened beside him, genuinely shocked.

David sighed. "I didn't know what I was saying but … you remember when we first came here? We didn't want to be witches or magicians. We hated it here!"

"That was before we knew about our powers."

"Yes. And now we're happy here. But that means we've changed, Jill. Maybe we've changed for the worse. Maybe we've become..."

"What?

"It doesn't matter."

But lying in bed, two hours later, David couldn't get the thought out of his mind. Had he become evil? It was true that he had cheated in the race and despite what Jill had said, he would have done anything to get his hands on the Unholy Grail. Even the name worried him. Unholy. Did it also describe him?

What is good and what is evil? Sometimes it's not as easy as you think to tell them apart...

He remembered what Mr Fitch (or was it Mr Teagle?) had said to him but he still wasn't sure what the head had meant. Good or evil? Stay or go? Why did everything have to be so complicated?

On the other side of the dormitory, Vincent turned in his sleep and pulled the sheets over him. David thought back to their first meeting. Vincent had arrived one July morning, carried over on the ferry that connected Skrull Island with the mainland. Handsome, athletic and quiet, Vincent seemed to fit in much faster than David had. In just a few weeks he had found his way through the mirror in the library and been given his own black ring. Maybe that was part of the trouble. The two of them had been in competition almost from the start and David had never bothered to find out anything about him; his home life, his parents, where he had come from.

How had he come to mistrust Vincent? Because of the East Tower. He had spotted Vincent coming out of the forbidden tower, next to the school's graveyard, and that had been the start of it. There was some sort of mystery connected with the place. Gregor knew. The school porter had stopped David going in.

David pushed his covers back and got out of bed. It was three o'clock in the morning; a cold, foggy night. He was probably mad. But he couldn't sleep anyway and he had nothing else to do. Whatever Vincent was really up to, he would find the answer in the East Tower. And he would go there now.

The night was bitterly cold. As David tiptoed through the school's graveyard his breath frosted and hung in the air around his head. Somewhere an owl hooted. A fat spider clambered down one of the gravestones and disappeared into the soil.

Something moved at the edge of the graveyard. David froze. But it was only a ghost, leaving its grave for a few hours' haunting. It hadn't seen him. Slowly, he moved on.

And there was the East Tower, looming out of the darkness ahead of him. David gazed at the crooked brickwork, the tangle of dark green ivy that surrounded it, the empty windows and, far above him, the broken battlements. He checked one last time. There was nobody around. He moved towards the entrance.

The only way into the East Tower was through a curved oak door, at least one metre thick. David was sure it would be locked but no sooner had he touched it than it swung inward, its iron hinges creaking horribly. There was something very creepy about the sound. For a moment he was tempted to go back to bed. But it was too late now. He had to settle this. He stepped inside.

The inner chamber of the tower was pitch black. A few tiny shafts of moonlight penetrated the cracks in the brickwork but the central area was a gaping hole. David didn't have a torch or even a box of matches with him. But he didn't need them. He closed his eyes and whispered a few words set down by the Elizabethan magician called John Dee. When he opened them again, the interior glowed with a strange green light. It was still gloomy but he could see.

The lower floor was empty, the ground strewn with rubble, a few nettles and poisonous herbs poking through. David sniffed the air. Although it was faint, there was something that he recognized, a smell that was at once familiar and yet strange. There was a sound somewhere high above, a sort of fluttering and a high-pitched whine. Ahead of him, a stone staircase climbed upwards, spiralling around on itself. David knew that the whole building was condemned, that any one of the stone slabs could crumble and send him crashing to certain death. But there was no other way. He had no choice.

He began to climb the stairs. The East Tower was fifty metres high. The staircase, pinned precariously to the outer wall, seemed to go on for ever and David was beginning to get dizzy when at last he found himself at the top. There was a coin in his trouser pocket and on an impulse he flicked it over his shoulder, into the hole at the centre of the stairs.

"One ... two ... three ... four ... five..."

It was a long time before the coin reached the bottom and tinkled on the concrete floor below.

Something moved. David heard a thin clatter like two pieces of cardboard being ruffled against each other. One step at a time, he moved across the concrete flagstones of the upper chamber. He had forgotten to put on any socks and he could feel the frozen air writhing around his ankles. For a second time he heard the strange, high-pitched whining. It was some sort of animal. What animal? What was this place?

He was in a completely circular room. Two of the narrow windows, quite close to each other, had mouldered, and now there was only a large, irregular gap. Opposite this, right up against the wall, there was a long wooden table with what looked like two or three baskets on top. Also on the table were an open book, a pile of paper, two candles, a quill pen and a leather-bound book.

David whispered three words. The candles ignited.

It was easier after that. David crossed over to the table and picked up one of the baskets. He felt something flutter between his hands. The front of the basket was a barred door, closed with a twist of wire. David looked inside and now saw what the animal was. A bat. Blind and frightened, it tried to fly, ricocheting off the sides of the cage.

What was Vincent doing with a collection of bats? David put down the cage and went over to the book. He scooped it up and examined it. It was an old exercise book, each page packed with writing so cramped and tiny that it was unreadable. David flicked through the pages. At last he arrived at a section he could read in the light of the candles. A poem:

> *Beware the shadow that is found*
> *Stretching out across the ground*
> *Where St Augustine once began*
> *And four knights slew a holy man*
> *For if the Grail is carried here*
> *Then Groosham Grange will disappear*

The Grail! Groosham Grange... What did it all mean?

David concentrated on the text. Saint Augustine. He was the man who had brought Christianity to England in the first century. But where had he begun? David racked his brain, trying to remember his history lessons with Miss Pedicure. Augustine had first landed in Thanet, Kent. But that wasn't right. Of course ... it was Canterbury! Canterbury Cathedral where four knights had slain Thomas à Becket in the reign of Henry II. Suddenly it was all crystal clear.

Carry the Unholy Grail into the shadow of Canterbury Cathedral and the school would disappear!

So that was what Vincent was planning. He wanted to destroy the school and had learned that the only way to do it was to get his hands on the Grail. But first he had to get rid of David – and he had done that brilliantly, baiting him to start with, then framing him and finally cheating him. In just three days' time, Vincent would be presented with his prize. And what then? Somehow he would smuggle it off the island. He would carry it to Canterbury. And then...

But what about the bats?

David put down the book and went over to the pile of paper. Paper, candles and bats. They were right next to each other. And when you added them together, what did you get? Candles to see by. Paper to write on. Bats to...

"Homing bats," he muttered. Why not? Homing bats were more reliable than homing pigeons. And they were perfect for carrying secret messages. They preferred the dark.

David felt in his trouser pocket and pulled out a pencil. It was such an old trick that he was almost ashamed to be trying it. Softly, he scribbled the pencil along the top sheet on the pile of paper, shading it grey. When he had pencilled over the entire sheet, he picked it up and held it against the candle flame.

It had worked. David could read five faint lines written in the same tight hand as the notebook:

EVEN MORE TOP SECRET THAN USUAL
To the Bishop of Bletchley

David Eliot is out of the running. The Grail
will be delivered on Prize-giving Day. Departure
from the island will proceed as planned. Am
confident that a few days from now, Groosham
Grange will no longer exist.

The note was signed with a cross.

Smiling to himself, David wandered over to the broken window and gazed out into the night. Just a few hours before, he had been considering packing his bags and leaving the school. Everything was different now. The sheet of paper and the notebook were all he needed. Once he showed them to the heads, the truth would come out.

What happened next took him completely by surprise. One moment he was standing on the edge of the tower. The next he was toppling forward as something – someone – crashed into the small of his back. He hadn't seen them. He hadn't heard them. For a second or two his hands flailed at the empty air. He tried to regain his balance but then whoever it was pushed him again and he fell out of the window, away from the tower, into the night.

He was dead. A fall of fifty metres on to the cold earth below would kill him for sure. The wind rushed into his face and the whole world twisted upside down. There was no time to utter a spell, no time to do anything.

With a last, despairing cry, he thrust his hand out, grabbing at the darkness, not expecting to find anything. But there was something. His fingers closed. Somehow his arm had caught a branch of ivy. He gripped tighter. He was still falling, pulling the ivy away with him as he went. But the further he fell, the thicker the ivy became. He was tangled up in it and it was slowing him down. More branches wrapped themselves around his chest and his waist. He came to a halt. With the ground only thirty metres away, the ivy reclaimed him, springing him back, crashing him into the brickwork. David shouted with pain. His arm had almost been torn out of its socket. But a few moments later he found himself dangling in mid-air. He was no longer falling. He was alive.

It took him thirty minutes to disentangle himself and climb the rest of the way down, and when he finally found himself on the ground once again he felt dizzy and sick. He took a deep breath, then looked back up. The window where he had been pushed was almost out of sight, terribly high up. It was a miracle that he was alive at all.

Even so, he knew what he had to do. As much as the idea appalled him, he had to be certain and so, forcing himself on, he went back into the East Tower and all the way back up the stairs. The top chamber was empty this time. And his worst fears had been realized. The pile of papers, the bats and the notebook were gone.

PRIZE-GIVING

The orange Rolls Royce was tearing up the motorway at a hundred miles an hour. All around it, cars were hooting, swerving and crashing into the hard shoulder as they tried to get out of the way.

"Shouldn't you be driving on the *left* side of the road, dear?" Mrs Eliot demanded.

"Nonsense," Mr Eliot replied, poking her with the cigarette lighter. "We're part of Europe now. I drive on the right in France and Switzerland. I don't see why I shouldn't do the same here."

Mrs Eliot's false eyelashes fluttered as an articulated lorry jackknifed out of their path, its horn blaring. "I think I'm going to be sick," she muttered.

"Well put your head out of the window," Mr Eliot snapped. "And this time remember to

261

open the window first."

Edward and Eileen Eliot were on their way to Norfolk in their specially converted Rolls Royce. Mr Eliot was unable to walk, which would have been sad except that he had never really liked walking in the first place and much preferred his wheelchair. He was a short, round man with more hair in his nostrils than on his head. His wife, Eileen, was much taller than him with so many false parts – hair, teeth, nails, eyelashes – that it was hard to be sure what she looked like at all.

They were not alone in the car. Wedged into the very corner of the back seat was a small, shrivelled woman in a drab cotton dress. She had pale cheeks, crooked teeth and hair that could have fallen off a horse. This was Mildred, Edward's sister. After eleven years of marriage, her husband had recently died of boredom. Mildred had talked all the way through the funeral and had only stopped when one of the undertakers had finally hit her with a spade.

"What's that funny rattling noise, Edward?" she asked now as the car turned off the motorway, went the wrong way round a roundabout and raced through a set of red lights.

"What rattling noise?" Mr Eliot demanded.

"I think it must be the engine," Mildred sniffed. "Personally I don't trust these English cars," she went on in her thin, whiny voice. "They're so unreliable. Why didn't you buy a nice Japanese car, Edward? The Japanese know how to build cars. Why didn't you...?"

"Unreliable!" Mr Eliot screamed, interrupting her. He wrenched the steering wheel, sending the car off the road and on to the pavement. "This is a Rolls Royce you're talking about! Do you know how much a Rolls Royce costs? It costs thousands! I didn't eat for a month after I bought my Rolls Royce. I couldn't afford petrol for three years!"

"They're very reliable," Eileen Eliot agreed, sticking her finger into the cigarette lighter to demonstrate. There was a flash as the dashboard short-circuited and she electrocuted herself.

"The Japanese couldn't build a Rolls Royce in a thousand years," Mr Eliot continued, unplugging his wife. "In fact they couldn't even pronounce it!" He jammed his foot down on the accelerator but he must have taken a wrong turning as he was now shooting through a playground with mothers and children hurling themselves into the flower-beds to get out of the way. "What sort of road is this?" he demanded, angrily.

"The Japanese have marvellous roads," Mildred remarked. "And bullet trains..."

"I'll bullet you..." Mr Eliot growled. He stamped down and the Rolls Royce smashed through a fence, leapt over the pavement and headed on towards the Norfolk coast.

Two hours later, they arrived.

Because it was on an island, Groosham Grange was unreachable by car – even by Rolls Royce – and the last part of the journey had to be undertaken by boat. Mr Eliot had parked right beside the sea and now he wheeled himself down to a twisting wooden jetty that jutted out precariously over the water. There was a boat waiting for them – an old fisherman's trawler. The old fisherman was sitting inside.

Seeing Mr Eliot, he stood up. "More parents?" he demanded.

Mr Eliot examined the man with distaste. He looked like something out of a pirate film, what with his black beard and single gold earring. "Yes," he said. "Will you ferry us over?"

"I will. I'll ferry you there. I'll ferry you back. I been doing it all day." The man spat. "Parents! Who needs 'em!"

"What's your name?" Mr Eliot demanded.

"Bloodbath. Captain Bloodbath." The captain squinted. "And I take it that's your lovely wife?"

Mr Eliot glanced at Mildred, who was standing beside him. She had a large, bulging handbag on her arm. "She's not my wife and she's not lovely," he replied. "My wife is under the car."

"I've fixed it!" Eileen Eliot called out and sat up, catching her head on the exhaust with a dull clang. There was oil on her dress and more on her face. She had a spanner in one hand and another one between her teeth. "I think you must have cracked a cylinder when you ran over that cyclist," she said, joining the others on the jetty.

"Typical English workmanship," Mildred muttered.

Mr Eliot took one of the spanners and hit her with it. "Let's get on the boat," he said.

A few minutes later, Captain Bloodbath cast off and, belching black smoke and rumbling, the boat began the crossing. The Captain sat at the front, steering, and Mr Eliot was surprised to see that his hands seemed to be made of steel.

"They're ally-minium!" Bloodbath exclaimed, noticing the banker staring at him. He clapped his hands together with a loud ping. "My own hands was pulled off last spring. Lost at sea. The boys made these ones for me in metalwork class. Very handy they are too!"

"Delightful," Mrs Eliot agreed with a weak smile.

There was a slight mist on the water but as they chugged forward, it suddenly parted. And there were the soaring cliffs of Skrull Island with the waves crashing and frothing on the jagged black rocks below. The boat pulled into a second jetty and then there was a five-minute drive up the steep road to the school with Gregor, who was simpering and sniggering at the wheel.

"I'm not sure I think too much of the staff," Mrs Eliot whispered. "I mean, that man with no hands! And unless I'm mistaken, this driver is completely deformed!"

The car stopped. Mildred uttered a little scream and leapt out.

"What's happened?" Mr Eliot exclaimed. "Has she been stung by a wasp?"

"It's David!" Mildred threw her hands up above her head. "Oh David! I hardly recognized you!" she warbled. She slapped her hands limply against her cheeks. "You've grown so tall! And you've put on weight! And your hair's so long. You've completely changed!"

"That's because I'm not David," the boy she was talking to said. "That's David over there..."

"Oh..."

By this time, Mr Eliot had been helped out of the car and he and Eileen Eliot were looking uncertainly at the school. The sun was shining and the whole building had been decked out for the day with a few strips of bunting and flags. A refreshment tent had been set up in the grounds.

But even so it still looked rather grim.

David walked over to them. "Hello, Mother," he said. "Hello, Father. Hello, Aunt Mildred."

Mr Eliot eyed his son critically. "How many prizes have you won?" he asked.

David sighed. "I'm afraid I haven't won any."

"Not any!" Mr Eliot exploded. "That's it then! Back in the car! We're going home."

"But we've only just got here," his wife protested.

Mr Eliot wheeled over her foot. "Well we're off again," he yelled. "I won a prize every year I was at Beton College. I won prizes for history, geometry and French. I even won prizes for winning prizes! If I hadn't won a prize, my father would have sliced me open with a surgical knife and confiscated one of my kidneys!"

By now Mr Eliot had gone bright red. He seemed to be having difficulty breathing and his whole face was contorted with pain. Mrs Eliot took out a bottle of pills and forced several of them into his mouth. "You shouldn't upset your father, David," she said. "You know he has trouble with his blood pressure. Sometimes his blood doesn't have any pressure at all!"

"I'm sorry," David muttered.

By the time Mr Eliot had recovered, Gregor had taken the car back to the jetty to fetch another batch of parents and so he was forced to stay. Fortunately for David, Mr Helliwell chose that moment to come over and introduce himself. The voodoo teacher was dressed in his smartest clothes for prize-giving: black suit and tails, wing collar and, perched on his head, a crooked, black hat. He had also painted his face white with black rings around his eyes. Both Mildred and Mrs Eliot trembled as he approached, but Mr Helliwell couldn't have been more friendly. "You should be very proud of David," he said.

"Why?" Mr Eliot asked.

"He's coming on very well." Mr Helliwell smiled, showing a line of teeth like tombstones. "He may have been unlucky, not getting the prize, but otherwise he's had a good year. I'm sure he'll get a good report."

David was grateful to the teacher despite himself. But he still couldn't meet Mr Helliwell's eyes. The memory of the trial and what had happened afterwards was still too raw.

"Perhaps you would like me to show you round the school," Mr Helliwell said.

"Round it?" Mrs Eliot asked. "Why can't we go in it?"

"He means in it, you idiotic woman," Mr Eliot snapped.

"This way…" Mr Helliwell winked at David and set off behind the electric wheelchair. Eileen

Eliot and Mildred followed.

"They have much more modern schools in Tokyo," Mildred said. She pulled her handbag further up her arm. "The Japanese have a wonderful education system…"

And then they were gone, entering the building through one of the open doors. They had quite forgotten David. But that suited him fine. The day was moving too fast. He needed time to think.

There were about thirty-five sets of parents on the island, more than eighty people in all, what with various aunts, uncles and friends. All of them were milling about in their best clothes, the women with hats and handbags, the men smug and smiling. Of course, they weren't going to be allowed to see everything. A lot of the school's equipment – the skulls, five-fingered candle-holders, wands, magic circles and the rest of it – had been hidden away. For the next ten minutes they would wander around the grounds and then they would all assemble in the marquee where Mr Kilgraw would make a speech and Vincent King would be awarded the Unholy Grail.

David knew that this would be the critical moment. It would be the only time when Vincent would have the Grail in his hands. If he was going to get it off the island, he would have to do it today.

And that was the one thing he still didn't know. How did Vincent plan to remove the Grail?

It seemed to him that there was only one way – in Captain Bloodbath's boat. But that had been kept well secured ever since David himself had stolen it a while back. So what was Vincent going to do? David had been surprised to discover that Vincent's parents weren't coming to prize-giving – so they couldn't take it for him. But perhaps he had someone in the crowd: a fake uncle or aunt. Perhaps the Bishop of Bletchley himself was here, in disguise. Even now he could be waiting to seize it. And with so many people coming and going, it would be easy to smuggle it away.

But David had no idea what the Bishop looked like – in disguise or out of it. There were plenty of parents with white hair and saintly faces. He could be any one of them. David glanced at the marquee. Vincent was standing in the sunlight with Monsieur Leloup, looking very dashing in a blazer and white trousers. The French teacher was introducing him to a group of parents, obviously flattering him. David felt a surge of jealousy. That should have been him.

"Seen anything?"

Jill had come up behind him and caught hold

of his arm. David had told her everything that had happened the morning after his fall from the East Tower. Only Jill, his closest friend on the island, would have believed him – and even she had taken a lot of persuading. But in the end she had agreed to help.

David shook his head. "No. Everything's so ordinary. But I know it's going to happen, Jill. And soon…"

"Maybe you should go to the heads, David."

"And tell them what?" David sighed. "They'd never listen to me."

"Look out!" Jill gestured in the direction of the school. "I think your parents are coming back."

"Do you want to meet them?"

"No thanks." Jill hurried off. She stopped a few paces away and turned round. "Don't worry, David," she said. "I'll keep an eye on Vincent."

Over by the marquee, Vincent glanced suddenly towards them. Had he overheard what she had just said?

But then Mr Helliwell reached David, still following his father in the wheelchair.

"An excellent school," Mr Eliot was saying. "I am most impressed. Of course, it is a little unnatural for boys and girls to be here together. At Beton College, where I went, there were only boys. In fact, even the headmaster's wife was a boy. But I suppose that's progress…"

"Absolutely," Mr Helliwell smiled politely. "Now if you'll excuse me…" The teacher hurried off towards the marquee.

Mr Eliot turned to his son. "Well, David," he said. "I can see it was a good decision to send you here."

"Your father does make wonderful decisions," Mrs Eliot agreed.

"I have suggested to Mr Helliwell a little more use of the cane," Mr Eliot went on. He nodded to himself. "What I always say is that a good beating never hurt anyone."

Mrs Eliot frowned. "But darling, if it didn't hurt, how could it be a good beating?"

"No, my love. What I mean is…"

But before Mr Eliot could either explain or demonstrate what he meant, a bell rang. The prize-giving was about to begin.

Mr and Mrs Eliot, Mildred and David joined the other parents. What with the narrow entrance and the number of people trying to get in, it was another quarter of an hour before they finally took their places. David looked around him, at the rows of seats stretched out underneath the canvas and the platform raised at the far end with the staff of Groosham Grange taking their places along it. He saw Vincent, sitting on his own. Then Mr Kilgraw stood up and everyone hushed.

But already there was something wrong. David looked one way, then another. Something had caught his eye. What was it? And then he saw, right at the back, near the entrance, an empty seat.

Mr Kilgraw had begun to speak but David didn't hear a word. He was scanning the audience, searching through the faces, the boys and the girls, the teachers and the parents...

But she wasn't there. The empty seat.

Jill had promised to keep an eye on Vincent. Vincent had overheard her. And now Jill had disappeared.

CRACKS

"Good afternoon, ladies and gentlemen," Mr Kilgraw began. The flaps had been drawn across the marquee to protect him from the sun, but just to be safe he was also wearing a slightly incongruous straw hat. "Welcome to Groosham Grange on this, our annual Prize-giving Day. May I begin by apologizing on behalf of the heads, Mr Fitch and Mr Teagle, who are unable to attend today. Mr Fitch has yellow fever. Mr Teagle has scarlet fever. If they get too close to each other, they go a nasty shade of orange.

"This has been a very successful year for Groosham Grange. Some might even say a magical year. I am pleased to tell you that our new biology laboratory has been built by workmen who were actually created in our old biology laboratory. Well done Lower Fifth! Our Ecology Group has been busy and we now have our own

Tropical Rain Forest on the south side of the island. Congratulations also to the Drama Group. They really brought *Frankenstein* to life. So, for that matter, did our physics class.

"It's not all work at Groosham Grange, of course. Our French class visited France. Our Ancient Greek class visited Ancient Greece. A school inspector visited us. And if you happen to pass through the cemetery, I hope you'll visit him. As usual, our staff has made many sacrifices. I would like to thank them and I ought also to thank the sacrifices…"

David found it hard to concentrate on what Mr Kilgraw was saying. He was sitting between his mother and father. Aunt Mildred, who was next to Edward Eliot, had already fallen asleep and was whistling softly through her nose. David was in the middle of the marquee, completely surrounded by parents: bald parents, fat parents, parents with red veins in their noses and wax in their ears, parents in expensive jewellery and expensive suits. He felt as if he was drowning in parents. Was this what he would be like one day? It was a horrible thought.

And it didn't make it any easier to think. David knew that the next few minutes would be critical. Once Vincent had the Unholy Grail, anything could happen. How would Vincent get the Grail off the island? Would he carry it himself, slipping away with the crowd? Or would he pass it to someone in the crowd – and if so, who? And what about Jill? David wanted to get up and look for her now but he knew that he couldn't. He was too close to Vincent. He was trapped.

"At Groosham Grange there is only one winner," Mr Kilgraw was saying. "And there is only one prize…"

David turned his attention back to the platform and saw that the assistant headmaster was holding something in his hands. Even from this distance he knew what it was. For the parents – bored and beginning to fidget – it was no more than a silver chalice decorated with red stones. But for David, the Unholy Grail seemed to glow with a light of its own. He could feel it reaching out to him. He had never wanted anything so much in his entire life.

"It is the school's most valued trophy," Mr Kilgraw went on. "In fact you could say that without it there would be no Groosham Grange. Every year it is presented to the student whose work, whose general behaviour and whose overall contribution to school life has put him or her at the top of the league. This year, the contest was particularly close…"

Was David imagining it or did Mr Kilgraw search him out, his eyes glittering as they locked into David's? It was almost a challenge. For the space of a heartbeat the two of them were alone beneath the canvas. The parents had gone. Vincent had gone. And David's hands twitched, reaching out to take what was rightfully his.

Then it was over.

"...but it gives me great pleasure to announce that the winner, our most distinguished pupil, is – Vincent King!"

David reluctantly joined in the general applause, at the same time trying to smile. Vincent stood up and went on to the stage. He shook hands with Mr Kilgraw. Mr Kilgraw muttered a few words. Vincent took the Grail and sat down again. The applause died away. And that was it. The Unholy Grail was his.

Mr Kilgraw spoke for another five minutes and David counted every one of them. The prize-giving might be over but he knew that his work was only beginning. Whatever happened, he intended to stick close to Vincent – and to the Grail. He would just have to worry about Jill later.

But it wasn't as easy as David had hoped. As soon as Mr Kilgraw had finished his speech, everyone stood up at once in a rush for the sherry and sausage rolls that Gregor and Mrs Windergast were serving at the back of the marquee. At the same time, Vincent was surrounded by people, examining the Grail and congratulating him, and it was as much as David could do to keep sight of him at all.

Worse than that, he still had his parents to deal with. Mr Eliot was in a bad mood. "I am disappointed," he was saying as he tore a sausage roll into shreds. "I wish I wasn't your father, to be frank. In fact I wish I was Frank's father. He won three prizes at Beton College."

"I just hope the neighbours don't find out," Mrs Eliot wept, gnawing at her fingers. "My own son! I can't bear it! We'll have to move. I'll change my name. I'll have plastic surgery…"

Aunt Mildred nodded in agreement. "My neighbour's children won *lots* of prizes," she announced. "But then, of course, they have a Japanese au pair…"

David craned his neck, searching for a gap between the three of them. The crowd that had formed around Vincent had separated again and suddenly Vincent had gone. David wasn't sure how he'd done it. But he had left the marquee.

Then Gregor limped over to them with a tray of food. "Sumfink tweet?" he gurgled.

"What?" Aunt Mildred asked.

"He's asking if you want something to eat," David translated. He glanced at the tray. "It's toad-in-the-hole," he said. "And I think Gregor's used real toads."

278

"I think it's time we went," Mildred whispered, going rather green.

Ten minutes later, David saw his parents into the car that would take them back down to the jetty and the boat.

"Goodbye, David," his father said. "I'm afraid I have not enjoyed seeing you. I can see now that your mother and I have always spoiled you."

"We ruined you," Mrs Eliot wept. Her make-up was flowing in rivers down her cheeks.

"I blame myself," Mr Eliot went on. "I should have beaten you more. My father beat me every day of my life. He used to buy cane furniture so that he could beat me with the chairs when he wasn't sitting on them. He knew a thing or two about discipline. Whack! Whack! Whack! That's all boys understand. Start at the bottom, that's what I say…"

"Don't excite yourself, dear," Mrs Eliot murmured.

Just then Aunt Mildred came running up to the car. "Sorry I'm late," she whined in her thin, nasal voice. "I couldn't find my handbag. Bye-bye, dear." She pecked David on the cheek. "Do come and visit me in Margate soon." She got into the car, heaving her handbag on to her lap. "I'm sure it wasn't as heavy as this when I set out this morning," she prattled on. "I can't think how I lost it. That nice teacher found it for me. Honestly, I'd forget my own head if it wasn't..."

She was still talking when Gregor started the car and they rattled off down the hill. David watched them until they were out of sight. Then he set off in the direction of the school.

Where could Vincent have gone?

David's first thought was the jetty but he decided not to go down there yet. He didn't want to follow his parents and the more he thought about it the less likely it was that Vincent would try to stow away on the boat. Captain Bloodbath was too careful – and anyway, it would be far easier to give the Grail to someone else and let them carry it for him. Vincent had to be somewhere in the school. David would find him and confront him with what he knew. But he had to move fast.

First he checked the marquee. The parents were starting to thin out, a few clusters of them still chatting with the staff, the rest walking with their sons and daughters towards the jetty. Mr Kilgraw had left. He would have gone inside to escape the sunlight. Mrs Windergast was still there, clearing away the food, and David went over to her.

"Excuse me," he said. "Have you seen Vincent?"

The matron smiled at him. "Not for a while, my dear. I suppose you want to congratulate him."

"Not exactly." David left the marquee.

In the next half hour he tried the library, the dormitory, the dining room, the hallways and the classrooms. He looked into the heads' study and Mr Kilgraw's study. Both rooms were empty. Then he tried the cemetery at the edge of the wood. There was no sign of Vincent.

David walked back to the school, feeling increasingly uncomfortable. Everything felt wrong. It was about two o'clock and the sun was shining but there was no warmth in the air, and no breeze, not even the faintest whisper of one. The light hitting the school was hard, unsparing. It was as if he had stepped out of real life and into a photograph, as if he were the only living thing.

He heard a sound high up, a faint rattling. He looked up, then blinked as something hit him on the side of the cheek. He rubbed the skin with the tips of his fingers. He had been hit by a pebble and a scattering of dust but he was unhurt. He squinted up in the direction of the sound. One wall of Groosham Grange loomed high above him, a grey gargoyle jutting out at the corner. There was a crack in the brickwork. It was only a small crack, zigzagging horizontally under the gargoyle, but David was sure it hadn't been there before. It looked too fresh, the edges pink against the grey surface of the bricks. It was no more than ten centimetres long. It was a crack, that was all.

But even as David lowered his head there was another soft rattle and a second shower of dust. He looked up again and saw that the crack had lengthened, curving up around the gargoyle. At the same time, a second crack had formed a few centimetres below. Even as he watched, a few pieces of mortar detached themselves from the wall and tumbled down to the earth below. And now there were three cracks, the longest about two metres and perhaps a centimetre wide. The gargoyle was surrounded by them. Its bulging eyes and twisted mouth almost looked afraid.

Suddenly David knew. He remembered the verse:

*For if the Grail is carried here
Then Groosham Grange will disappear*

The disappearance of Groosham Grange had begun.

The Unholy Grail had already left the island.

The question was, had Vincent gone with it? David knew that he had to find the other boy fast. How far away was Canterbury? He had no doubt that the Grail was already on its way there. Perhaps it was already too late.

But with the onrush of panic came another thought. He had forgotten to look in the one place where he was most likely to find Vincent, the one place that had been tied in with the mystery from the start: the East Tower. Even if the Grail had gone, Vincent might be hiding out there and if he could just find Vincent he might yet be able to recapture the Grail. David broke into a run. As he went, a fourth, larger crack opened up in the wall just beside his head.

He reached the door of the tower and without stopping to think, kicked it open and ran in. After the brightness of the afternoon light, the darkness inside the building was total. For about five seconds David was completely blind and in that time he realized three things.

First, that Vincent had been there recently. There was a smell in the air, the same smell that David had noticed the night he had nearly been killed.

Second, that he should have gone in more cautiously and allowed his eyes time to get used to the darkness.

And third, that he was not alone.

The hand that reached out and grabbed him by the throat was invisible. Before he could utter a sound a second hand clamped itself over his mouth. This hand was holding a pad of material soaked in something that smelled of rotting fruit and alcohol. And as David choked and struggled and slipped into unconsciousness, he thought to himself that the hand was very big, surely far too big to belong to Vincent.

But if it wasn't Vincent, who on earth could it be?

VINCENT

David's arms, wrists and shoulders were hurting. It was the pain that woke him – that and someone calling his name. He opened his eyes and found himself hunched up on the floor with his back against the wall of a room that he recognized. He was in the upper chamber of the East Tower. Somebody had knocked him out, carried him upstairs, tied him up and left him there.

But who?

All along he had been certain that Vincent King was his secret enemy and that it had been Vincent who was plotting to steal the Grail. Now, at last, he knew that he had been wrong. For there was Vincent right opposite him, also tied up, his hair for once in disarray and an ugly bruise on the side of his face. Jill was sitting next to him, in a similar state. She was the one calling to him.

David straightened himself. "It's all right," he said. "I'm awake."

He tried to separate his wrists but it was impossible. They were tied securely behind his back with some sort of rough rope. He could feel it cutting into his flesh and it was as much as he could do to wiggle his fingers. He pushed himself further up against the wall, using the heel of his shoe against the rough flagstones. "Just give me a few seconds," he said. He shut his eyes again and whispered the first few words of a spell that would bring a minor Persian demon to his assistance.

"Forget it," Vincent cut in and David stopped in surprise. The other boy had hardly ever talked to him. Usually they did their best to avoid each other. But now it seemed that they were on the same side. Even so, Vincent sounded tired and defeated. "If you're trying some magic, it won't work," he said. "I've already tried."

"Look at the door," Jill said.

David twisted his head round uncomfortably. There was a shape painted on the closed door. It looked like an eye with a wavy line through it.

"It's the eye of Horus," Vincent said. "It creates a magical barrier. It means…"

"…it means we can't use our powers," David

concluded. He nodded. "I know."

Gritting his teeth, he see-sawed his wrists together, trying to loosen the rope. It cost him a few inches of skin and gave him little in return. His hands had rotated and his palms could meet. He might have been able to pick up something if there was anything in the tower to pick up. But that was all.

He gave up. "Who did this?" he asked.

Vincent shook his head. "I don't know. I never saw them."

"Nor me," Jill added. "I was following Vincent like you said. But just before the prize-giving started, I decided to take a quick look in here. Someone must have been waiting. I didn't see anything."

"Nor did I," David muttered, gloomily.

"Why *were* you following me?" Vincent asked.

Jill jerked her head in David's direction. She was unable to keep a sour tone out of her voice. "He thought you were going to steal the Grail."

Vincent nodded briefly. "That figures," he muttered.

"I knew *someone* was going to steal the Grail," David said. He was blushing again. He had been wrong from the start, horribly wrong, and his mistake could end up killing all of them. He thought back now, remembering everything that had happened. And the words poured out.

287

"I was set up that night in the heads' study. I was never trying to steal the exam. And I did know what thanatomania means. Somebody stole part of my answer. And what about the waxworks? OK – maybe it wasn't you who sent them after me, but I wasn't making it up. Somebody stole the statuette so that you could win." David realized he wasn't making much sense. He slumped back into silence.

"Is that why you were against me from the start?" Vincent asked.

"I wasn't…"

"You never gave me a chance."

David knew it was true. He wasn't blushing because he had been wrong but because he had been cruel and stupid. He had thought the worst of Vincent for the simple reason that he didn't like him, and he didn't like him because the two of them had been in competition. Vincent was right. David had never given him a chance. They had been enemies from the start.

"How was I to know?" David muttered. "I didn't know you…"

"You never asked," Vincent said. There was a pause and he went on. "I didn't want to come here," he said. "I didn't have any parents. My dad left when I was a kid and my mother didn't want to know. They put me in an institution … St Elizabeth's in Sourbridge. It was horrible.

Then I got moved here." He took a deep breath. "I thought I'd be happy at Groosham Grange, especially when I found out what was really going on. All I wanted was to be one of you, to be accepted. I didn't even care about the Unholy Grail."

"I'm sorry..." David had never felt more ashamed.

"I did try to be friends with you, but everything I did just made it worse." He sighed. "Why did you think it was me? Why me?"

"I don't know." David thought back. "I saw you coming out of the tower," he said, knowing how lame it sounded. "And that night, when I was caught looking at the exam papers ... did you come here then?"

Vincent nodded. "Yes."

"Why?"

Vincent thought for a moment, then answered. "I smoke," he said. "I started smoking cigarettes when I was at Sourbridge and I've never given up."

"Smoking!" David remembered the smell. He had come across it twice but he hadn't recognized it: stale tobacco smoke. "I don't believe it!" he said. "Smoking is mad. It kills you. How can you be so stupid?"

"You've been pretty stupid too," Jill muttered.

David fell silent. "Yes," he agreed.

Vincent struggled with his ropes. "I suppose it's a bit late now to think about giving up."

The words were no sooner spoken than there was a distant rumble, soft and low at first but building up to a sudden crash. David looked out of the window. The sky was grey, but it wasn't the colour of nightfall. It was an ugly, electric grey, somehow unnatural. There was a storm closing in on Skrull Island and sitting high up in the tower, right in the middle of it, he felt very uncomfortable indeed.

"I think..." he began.

He got no further. The whole tower suddenly trembled as if hit by a shockwave and at the same moment Jill cried out. A great chunk of wall right next to her simply fell away leaving a gap above her head. Outside, the air swirled round in a dark vortex and rushed into the room. There was a second crash of thunder. The chamber shook again and a crack appeared in the floor between David and Vincent, the heavy flagstones ripping apart as if they were made of paper.

"What's happening?" Jill cried.

"The Grail's left the island," David shouted. "It's the end..."

"What are we going to do?" Vincent said.

David glanced at the door, at the symbol painted in white on the woodwork. Even if he could have reached the eye of Horus, he would have been unable to rub it out. But while it was there, there was no chance of any magic. If they were going to escape, they would have to use their own resources. He searched the floor, trying not to look at the crack. There were no broken bottles, no rusty nails, nothing that would cut through the rope. Opposite him, Vincent was struggling feverishly. He had worked his hands loose but his wrists were still securely tied.

A third crash of thunder. This time it was the roof that was hit. As Jill screamed and rolled on her side to protect herself, two wooden rafters crashed down, followed by what felt like a tonne of dust and rubble. Vincent completely disappeared from sight and for a moment David thought he had been crushed. But then Vincent coughed and staggered on to his knees, still fighting with his ropes.

"The whole place is falling apart!" Jill shouted. "How high up are we?"

"Too high up," David shouted back. The crack in the floor had widened again. Quite soon the entire thing would give way and all three of them would fall into a tunnel of broken stone and brickwork with certain death fifty metres below.

Then he had a thought. "Vincent!" he called out. "After the prize-giving you came in here to have a cigarette."

"Yes," Vincent admitted. "But don't tell me it's bad for my health. Not now!"

"You've got cigarettes on you?"

"David, this is no time to take it up," Jill wailed.

"Yes," Vincent said.

"What were you going to light them with?"

Vincent understood at once. For the first time, David found himself admiring the other boy and knew that if only they'd been working together from the start, none of this would have happened. Contorting his body, Vincent spilled the contents of his pockets on to the floor: a handful of coins, a pen, a cigarette lighter.

Moving with his hands tied behind his back wasn't easy. First he had to turn himself round, then grope behind him to pick up the lighter. At the same time, David shuffled across the floor, pushing himself with his feet. He stopped at the crack, feeling the floor move. Jill cried out a warning. David threw himself forward. The thunder reverberated all around – closer this time – and a whole section of the floor, the section where David had just been sitting, fell away leaving a jagged black hole. David crashed down, almost dislocating his shoulder. Far below, he heard the flagstones shatter at the bottom of the tower and breathed a sigh of relief that he hadn't fallen with them.

"Hurry!" Vincent urged him.

Bruised and aching, David manoeuvred himself so that he was back to back with the other boy. For her part, Jill had edged closer to them. The whole chamber was breaking up. Nowhere was safe. But if one went, all would go. There was some sort of comfort in that.

"This is going to hurt," Vincent said.

"Do it," David said.

Fumbling with his fingers, afraid he would drop it, Vincent flicked the lighter on. He had to work blind, sitting with his back to David, and there was no time to be careful. David felt the flame of the lighter sear the inside of his wrist and shouted out in pain.

"I'm sorry..." Vincent began.

"It's not your fault. Just keep going."

Vincent flicked the lighter back on, trying to direct the flame to where he thought the ropes must be. The wind was rushing into the chamber through the holes in the wall and ceiling. David could hear it racing round the tower. He winced as the lighter burnt him once again but this time he didn't cry out. He was grateful the flame hadn't blown out.

More brickwork fell. Jill had gone white and David thought she was going to faint, but then he saw that falling plaster had covered her from head to toe. Jill wasn't the fainting sort. "I can smell burning," she said. "It must be the rope."

"Unless it's me," David muttered.

He was straining his arms, trying to avoid the flame. It felt as if he had been sitting there for ever. But then there was a jerk and his hands parted. Another few seconds and he was standing up, free, the two ends of the singed rope hanging from his wrists. Next, he released Vincent. The cigarette lighter had badly burned the other boy's thumb and the side of his hand. David could see the red marks. But Vincent hadn't complained.

Then it was Jill's turn. With Vincent's help, the ropes came away quickly and then the three of them were racing across the floor even as it fell away beneath them. Soon there would be nothing left of the tower. It was as if there were some invisible creature inside the storm, devouring the stone and mortar.

David reached the door first. It was unlocked. Whoever had tied them up had been confident about their knots. Clinging on to Jill, with Vincent right behind him, David made his way down the spiral staircase. About halfway down, two more flagstones fell past, narrowly missing them before shattering with an explosive crash. But the lower parts of the tower were holding up. The further they went, the safer they became. They reached the bottom unharmed.

But when they emerged into the open air, everything had changed.

Skrull Island was black, lashed by a stinging acid rain. The clouds writhed and boiled like something in a witch's cauldron. The wind stabbed at them, hurling torn plants and grass into their faces. There was nobody in sight. To one side, the cemetery looked wild and derelict with several of its gravestones on their sides. Groosham Grange itself looked dark and dismal, like some abandoned factory. A lattice-work of cracks had spread across it. Many of its windows had been smashed. The ivy had been torn away and hung down, a tangled mess. There was a flash of lightning and one of the gargoyles separated from the wall, launching itself into the blackness of the sky with an explosion of broken plaster.

"The Grail…" Vincent began.

"It's begun its journey south," David shouted. "If it reaches Canterbury, that'll be it…!"

"But who took it?" Jill demanded. "If it wasn't Vincent, who was it?"

"And what can we do?" Vincent held up a hand to protect his eyes from the hurtling wind. "We've got to get it back…!"

"I don't know!" David cried.

But suddenly he did know. Suddenly a whole lot of things had fallen into place. He knew who had the Grail. He knew how it had been smuggled off the island. The only thing he didn't know was how he could possibly reach it.

Then Vincent grabbed his arm. "I've got an idea," he yelled.

"What?"

"We can get off the island. One of us..."

"Show me!" David said.

The thunder crashed again. The three of them turned and ran into the school.

PURSUIT

It was getting very hot inside the Rolls Royce.

Mr Eliot ran a finger round his collar and flicked on the on-board computer showing the engine temperature. The engine's heat was normal but he was sweating. His wife was sweating. Even the leather upholstery was sweating. In the back seat, all Aunt Mildred's make-up had run and she now looked like a Sioux Indian in a rainstorm. It was very odd. The sun was shining but it was already late in the day. How could it be so warm?

"I think I'm going to faint," Mrs Eliot muttered and promptly did, her head crashing into the dashboard.

"Oh no!" Mr Eliot wailed.

"Is she hurt?" Mildred asked, clutching her handbag tightly to her chest and peering over the seat.

"I don't know," Mr Eliot replied. "But she's cracked the walnut panelling. Do you know how much that panelling cost me? It cost me a fortune! It's made out of South American walnuts!"

"I think she's dead," Mildred whispered.

Mr Eliot poked his wife affectionately in the ear. "No. She's still breathing," he said.

By now all the windows in the Rolls Royce had steamed up which, as they were still driving at ninety miles per hour down the motorway, made things rather difficult. But Mr Eliot still clung grimly to the steering wheel, overtaking on the inside and swerving on the outside. At least he was driving on the correct side of the road.

"Why don't you turn on the air conditioning?" Aunt Mildred suggested.

"Good thinking!" Mr Eliot snarled. "Pure mountain air. That's what you get in a Rolls Royce. In fact I could have bought a mountain for the amount it cost me."

"Just do it, dear," Mildred panted as her lipstick trickled over her chin.

Mr Eliot pressed a button. There was a roar and before either of them could react they were engulfed in a snow-storm that rushed at them through the air-conditioning vents, filling the interior of the car. In seconds their sweat had frozen. Long icicles hung off Mr Eliot's nose and chin. His moustache had frozen solid. The intense cold had the effect of waking Mrs Eliot up but by now her face had stuck to the surface of the dashboard. On the back seat, Aunt Mildred had virtually disappeared beneath a huge snow drift that rose over her like a white blanket. The Rolls Royce swerved left and right, sending a Fiat and a Rover hurtling into the crash barrier. Mr Eliot's hands were now firmly glued to the steering wheel.

"What's going on?" he screamed, his breath coming out in white clouds. "I had the car serviced before I left. It was a Rolls Royce service man. And all Rolls Royce service men are regularly serviced themselves. What's happening? This is motorway madness!"

"There's a service station," Aunt Mildred whimpered. "Why don't we stop for a few minutes?"

"Good idea!" Mr Eliot agreed and wrenched the car over to the left.

It took them ten minutes to extract themselves from the frozen Rolls Royce, which they left to thaw slowly in the sun. Eileen Eliot had to be chiselled off the dashboard and then had to use a blowtorch to separate Edward Eliot from the steering wheel, but eventually the three of them were able to make their way up the concrete ramp that led to the Snappy Eater café.

The Snappy Eater was a typical English motorway restaurant. The tables were plastic. The chairs were plastic. And the food tasted of plastic. A few motorists were sitting in the brightly coloured room, surrounded by artificial flowers, listening to the piped music and miserably nibbling their luke-warm snacks. Outside, the traffic roared past and the smell of burning tyres and petrol hung heavy in the air.

Mildred looked round her and sniffed. "They have wonderful service stations in Japan," she muttered. "You can get marvellous sushi..."

"What's sushi?" Eileen asked. She was feeling rather car-sick.

"It's raw fish!" Mildred explained enthusiastically. "Lovely strips of raw fish, all wet and jelly-like. All the Japanese motorway restaurants have them."

"Oh God!" Mrs Eliot gurgled and ran off in the direction of the toilet.

"I love Japanese food," Mildred continued, sitting down at a table and heaving her handbag in front of her.

"Why don't you shut up about Japan, you interfering old goat?" Mr Eliot asked as he wheeled himself next to her. He snatched the menu. "Here. They've got battered cod and chips. You can have that raw. Better still, you can have it battered. I'll batter you myself..."

A few minutes later, Eileen Eliot returned and they ordered two plates of vegetarian spaghetti and one portion of cod. But things had already begun to change inside the Snappy Eater.

Nobody noticed anything at first. The roar of the traffic drowned out the screams of the children who had been playing outside on a slide shaped like a plastic dragon. But the dragon was no longer plastic. It had already swallowed two of the children and was chasing a third with very real claws and fiery breath. About fifty metres away, at the garage, motorists dived for cover as several of the pumps fired high-velocity bullets in all directions. Instead of serving unleaded petrol, it seemed the pumps had decided to give out unpetrolled lead.

Inside the restaurant, the piped music was still oozing out of the speakers – but now it really *was* oozing out. It was dripping down like honey, only bright pink and much stickier. The plastic flowers were being attacked by plastic wasps. All the waiters and waitresses had broken out in spots. The one who was serving the Eliots had lost all his hair as well.

"Oh goodness!" Mildred exclaimed as her meal was set in front of her. "This cod is swimming in grease!"

And it was. It appeared that the chef had

neglected to kill it and the silvery fish was happily swimming in a large bowl of cold grease.

"I'm not sure about this spaghetti..." Eileen Eliot began. But the spaghetti was also not sure about her. It had come alive. Like an army of long, white worms, it slithered and jumped out of the bowl and, giggling to itself, raced across the table top.

The same thing had happened to Mr Eliot's. "Get back on my plate!" he demanded, jabbing at the table with a fork. But the spaghetti ignored him, hurrying away to join two naked and headless chickens that had just escaped from the kitchen, running out on their drumsticks.

"This place is a madhouse!" Mr Eliot said. "Let's get out of here!"

Eileen and Mildred agreed, but even leaving the restaurant wasn't easy. The revolving doors were revolving so fast that walking into them was like walking into a food processor, and two policemen and a lorry driver had already been shredded. But eventually they found a fire exit and made their way round to the carpark where their car was waiting.

"This would never happen in Japan," Mildred exclaimed.

"I'll put her in the boot!" Mr Eliot muttered

as he started the engine. "I wish I'd never brought her..."

"What is going on?" Eileen Eliot moaned.

The Rolls Royce reversed over somebody's picnic and into a wastepaper basket. "Margate, here we come!" Mr Eliot cried.

Mildred Eliot sat miserably on the back seat with her handbag beside her. Although she hadn't noticed it and probably wouldn't have mentioned it if she had, the handbag had begun to glow with a strange green light. And there was something inside it, humming softly and vibrating.

The Rolls Royce swerved back on to the motorway and continued its journey south.

David clung on for dear life, suspended between the ocean bubbling below and the storm clouds swirling above. Every gust of wind threatened to knock him off his perch and the wind never stopped. There wasn't a muscle in his body that wasn't aching and yet he couldn't relax, not for an instant. He had to concentrate. With his hands clamped in front of him, his arms rigid, his face lashed by the rain, he urged the broomstick on.

It had been Vincent's idea.

Mrs Windergast's broomstick was the only way off the island. Even if they had been able to take Captain Bloodbath's boat, the sea was far too rough for sailing. Mrs Windergast had taught them the basic theory of broomstick flying. True, they had never tried it before and certainly not in a full-blown storm. But as soon as Vincent had suggested it, David knew it was the only way.

They had taken the broomstick from Mrs Windergast's room. Normally the door would have been locked and the room would certainly have been protected by a magic spell. But everything had changed in the storm. The staff and pupils had vanished, taking shelter in the caverns below while the elements – the sea, the wind, the lightning and the rain – joined forces to destroy the island. Mrs Windergast's room was empty but one of the windows had been shattered and pools of water and broken glass covered the carpet. There were papers everywhere. The curtains flapped madly against the wall. The broomstick lay on its side, half hidden by a chair.

"You know where you're going?" Jill called out. She had to raise her voice to make herself heard above the storm.

David nodded. A half-remembered line here and a few spoken words there had come together and everything had clicked. He had worked it out.

His parents. After they left Groosham Grange

they were taking Mildred back to her home in Margate. Edward Eliot had told him as much in the letter he had written a few weeks before. And where was Margate? Just a few miles north of Canterbury.

And what had Aunt Mildred said as she got into the car? *I'm sure it wasn't as heavy as this when I set out...* She had lost her handbag. It had been handed back to her – but heavier than before. David was certain. Somebody had hidden the Grail inside the handbag. And she had unwittingly carried it off the island.

Clutching the broomstick in Mrs Windergast's room, David knew that he had to fly south, somehow find the orange Rolls Royce and intercept it before it reached Margate. Someone would be waiting for it at the other end. But who? That was still a mystery.

"Be careful," Vincent said. "It's not as easy as it looks."

"And hurry, David," Jill added. "The school's powers are failing. If the Grail gets too close to Canterbury, the broomstick won't fly. You'll fall. You'll be killed."

Feeling slightly ridiculous, David pushed the broomstick between his legs with the twigs poking out behind. How had Mrs Windergast done it? He concentrated and almost at once felt the stick pushing upwards. His feet left the floor and then he wasn't exactly flying but wobbling above the carpet, trying to keep his balance.

"Good luck," Vincent said.

David turned round in mid-air. "Thanks," he said. Then he and the broomstick lurched out of the window and into the storm.

The first few minutes were the worst. The wind seemed to be coming at him from all directions, invisible fists that punched at him again and again. The rain blinded him. He knew he was climbing higher but in what direction, north or south, he couldn't say. The broomstick worked through some sort of telepathy. He only had to think "right" to go that way. But if he thought too hard, the broomstick would spin round like a fairground ride and it was as much as he could do to hang on. He glimpsed Groosham Grange, rising at a crazy angle in the corner of his eye. Then it was upside-down! He had to get his bearings. He felt sick and exhausted and the journey hadn't even begun. He forced the broomstick up the right way. With his body tensed, he resisted the force of the storm. He was about a hundred metres up. And at last he had control.

And so he flew. The broomstick had no speed limit and seemed to have left the island behind in only seconds. The Norfolk coastline was already visible ahead. He relaxed, then yelled out as he collided with a flock of seagulls. Again he was blinded, aware only of grey feathers and indignant cries all around him. The control was broken and the broomstick plunged down, pulling David after it, his stomach lurching. The sea rushed up to swallow him.

"Up!" David shouted and thought it too, clamping his mind on it. Despite everything, he didn't panic. Already he understood that panic would freeze his mind and without a clear mind he couldn't fly. He relaxed everything, even his hands. And at once the broomstick responded. It had swooped down but now it curved gently up. The sea had gone. As the broomstick rose higher, David saw dry land below, the sandy beaches of the Norfolk coast. He had left the storm behind him. The sun was shining.

Swallowing hard, he turned the broomstick south and set off in pursuit of the Unholy Grail.

After David had gone, Vincent and Jill left Mrs Windergast's room and made their way downstairs, heading for the network of underground caves beneath the school. The wind was still howling outside and as they reached the main staircase a huge stained-glass window suddenly exploded inwards, showering them with multi-coloured fragments of glass. They ran into the library, intending to pass through the mirror that concealed the passage down – but the windows in the room had been shattered by the storm and the mirror had broken too. A single crack ran down its face, effectively sealing it. Jill knew that if they tried to pass through a cracked mirror, they would be cut in half.

"Outside!" Vincent shouted. Jill nodded and followed him.

It was even worse outside than they had imagined. The entire island was in the grip of something like a volcanic eruption. Whole trees had been torn up, the gravestones in the cemetery blown apart, the larger tombs thrown open. The sky was midnight black, crossed and re-crossed by streaks of lightning that were like razor blades slashing at the air. The whole of the East Tower had collapsed in on itself. The rest of the school looked as if it was about to do the same.

"Look!" Jill pointed and Vincent followed her finger to the gargoyles that surrounded Groosham Grange. Their eyes were shining, bright red in the darkness, like warning lights before a nuclear explosion. At the same time, something huge and terrifying was rising up in the far distance behind the school. Jill had only just seen what it was before Vincent had grabbed her, throwing her into the safety of one of the tombs.

It was a tidal wave. The whole world disappeared in a silver-grey nightmare as the wave pounded down on the school, completely engulfing the cemetery, the wood, everything. A second later, the ground was shaken by some awful convulsion below and Jill found herself thrown into Vincent's arms.

"How much longer?" she cried. "How much more can the school take?"

Vincent had gone quite pale. He was cold and soaking wet, drenched by the water that had found its way into the tomb. "I don't know," he said. "The Grail must be getting closer to Canterbury." He looked up into the pitch-black sky. "Come on, David," he whispered. "We're running out of time."

The power of the Unholy Grail was growing steadily. And it was becoming more unpredictable and more out of control the further it was taken from Groosham Grange.

"I feel very peculiar," Mildred was saying. "It must be something I ate. I'm blowing up all over."

Eileen Eliot turned round and looked into the back of the car. The small, shrivelled woman was expanding as if someone had connected her to an air hose. Her handbag lay next to her, humming and glowing brilliantly. Mildred's shoulders and chest had torn through her clothes and she had lost a great deal of her hair. There was also something rather odd about her eyes. "It's true, Edward," Eileen squeaked. "I think we'd better take her to a doctor."

But Edward Eliot ignored her. He himself had changed during the last few minutes. His skin had become thicker, pinker. His hands and face were covered unevenly with bristles and his ears and nose had changed shape.

"Edward...?" Eileen quavered.

Mr Eliot snorted and stamped his foot down on the accelerator. Except he no longer had a foot. His shoe had come off to reveal what looked remarkably like a pig's trotter.

Eileen Eliot slumped in her seat and began to cry. All around her, the entire world was bending and twisting out of shape as the familiar turned into the insane.

One moment they were approaching a zebra crossing. Then the air seemed to shimmer and a moment later a whole herd of zebras had emerged in a stampede from a post office. Cat's eyes set in the tarmac disappeared as the cats – panthers, jaguars and tigers – leapt out to terrorize the unfortunate people of Margate. Pelican lights sprouted wings and flew off. A humpback bridge spouted a great spray of water before being harpooned by a party

310

of Icelandic tourists.

Inside the handbag, the Unholy Grail hummed and glimmered.

Mildred's dress tore in half. She was enormous now and when she spoke again, it was not English that came out of her lips. It was Japanese. Her cheeks bulged and her great, fat legs stuck out like tree stumps.

Eileen Eliot realized what had happened. Aunt Mildred had always loved the Japanese. Now she had become one. A sumo wrestler.

"Edward..." she wept.

Mr Eliot snorted again. He was no longer able to speak. His mouth and nose had moulded themselves together and jutted forward over what was left of his chin. His teeth had also doubled in size. The sleeves of his jacket and shirt had torn open to reveal two pink, knotted arms, covered in the same spiky hair that bristled out of his neck and face.

Edward Eliot had always been a road-hog. And so the Unholy Grail had turned him into one.

Eileen Eliot took one look at him and screamed. "This can't be happening!" she whimpered. "It's horrible. Horrible! I wish I was ten thousand miles from here."

The Unholy Grail heard her. There was a sudden *whoosh!* and she felt herself being sucked out of the car in a tunnel of green light, her clothes being torn off as she went. For a few seconds the whole world disappeared. Then she was falling, screaming all the way. The ground rushed up at her and the next thing she knew she was standing in a pool of cold and muddy water that reached up to her waist.

Mrs Eliot had travelled thousands of kilometres. She was standing in a paddy field in China, surrounded by some very surprised Chinese rice farmers. Mrs Eliot smiled and fainted.

Mr Eliot had seen his wife disappear. He turned and stared at the empty seat ... not a good idea at seventy miles per hour. The next thing he knew, the car had left the road and crashed into a lamppost. Of course he hadn't bothered with a seat-belt and he was hurled, snorting and squealing, through the very expensive smoked-glass front window, out on to the pavement. Wedged in the back, her huge stomach trapped by the front seat, Aunt Mildred was unable to move. But at least her flesh had cushioned her from the impact.

The back door of the Rolls Royce had been torn open in the collision and Mildred's handbag had rolled out. It lay on the pavement, glowing more powerfully than ever. Awkwardly, Mildred poked an arm out and tried to reach it. But before her podgy fingers could close on the bag, someone appeared, leaning down to snatch it away.

Mildred gazed at the figure in astonishment. "You!" she said.

But then the person had gone. And the handbag had gone too.

Far below him, David could see the chaos that was the centre of Margate and knew with a surge of excitement that he was getting closer. He was flying at two hundred metres – high enough, he hoped, not to be seen from the ground but low enough to avoid any passing planes. He had had one nasty fright as he had crossed the Thames Estuary at Sheerness and a DC10 taking off from City Airport had cut right in front of him. There had also been some unpleasant air currents to negotiate over the flat Suffolk countryside. But he was almost there. He had done it.

But the worst surprise was still to come.

David had flown inland, leaving Margate behind him. He was actually beginning to enjoy the journey, the rush of the wind in his hair, the complete silence, the sense of freedom as he soared through the late afternoon sunlight. The broomstick was responding instantly to the slightest suggestion. Up, down, left, right – he only had to think it and he was away.

Then suddenly it stopped.

David's stomach lurched as the broomstick plummeted down and it was only by forcing his thoughts through his clenched hands and into the wooden shaft that he was able to regain control. The broomstick continued forward but more hesitantly. Then it shuddered and dipped again. David knew his worst fear had been realized. Just as Jill had warned, the Grail was approaching Canterbury. And the closer it got, the less powerful he became. Groosham Grange with all its magic was falling apart – and that included the broomstick. It was like a car running out of petrol. He could actually feel it coughing and stammering beneath him. How much further could he go?

And then he saw the cathedral. It stood at the far end of a sprawling modern town, separated from it by a cluster of houses and a swathe of perfectly mown grass. The cathedral stretched from east to west, a glinting pile of soaring towers, arched windows and silver-white roofs that looked, from this height, like some absurdly expensive Hornby model. It was there, only a few kilometres away. David urged the broomstick on. It surged obediently forward but then dropped another fifty metres. David could feel its power running out.

The broomstick reached the High Street of

Canterbury and followed it up and over the elegant Christ Church Gate and past the cathedral itself. David found himself high above the central tower. Looking down, he could see right into the cloisters. He could hear organ music drifting through the stone walls. Leaning to one side, he tilted round, looking for somewhere to land.

And that was when the broom's power failed. There was nothing he could do. Like a wounded bird he fell out of the sky, spinning round and round, still clinging to the useless broomstick that was now above his head. The cathedral had disappeared, whipped out of his field of vision. He could see the grass rushing up at him, a solid green wall.

David turned once in the air, cried out, then hit the ground and lay still.

CANTERBURY CATHEDRAL

He was still alive. He knew because of the pain. David wasn't sure how many bones there were in the human body but it felt as if he had broken every one of them. He was surprised he could even move.

He was lying on the grass like one of those chalk drawings you get after a murder. His arms and legs were sticking out at strange angles. His head was pounding and he could taste blood where he had bitten his tongue. But he was still breathing. He guessed that at the last minute the broomstick must have slowed his fall. Otherwise he wouldn't have been on the grass – he would have been underneath it.

He opened his eyes and looked around him. He had landed in the very middle of the cathedral close. On one side of him there was a wooden building – the Cathedral Welcome

Centre – and a couple of trees. Behind there was a row of houses that included the Cathedral Shop. The cathedral itself was in front of him, above him, looming over him.

It began with two towers that at some time had become home to a family of black, ragged birds. Ravens or crows perhaps. They were swooping in and out of the pointed windows, launching themselves into the sky. Then there were two lines of smaller towers, so intricately carved that they looked like something that might have grown at the bottom of the sea. At the far end there was a taller tower. It stood poised like a medieval rocket about to be launched. The sun was trapped behind it, low in the sky.

The sun...

With an effort, David sat up and saw that this third tower was casting a shadow that stretched out across the lawn, stopping only a few metres from where he lay. At the same time, he saw somebody moving towards him.

The solitary figure walked steadily forward. David squinted, raising himself on his arm. The pain made him cry out but he still couldn't see who it was. He was blinded by the light shafting into his eyes and he was still dizzy and disorientated after his fall.

"Hello, David," Mr Helliwell said.

Mr Helliwell.

He should have known all along.

David had suspected Vincent because Vincent was new. But so was Mr Helliwell. He had joined the staff at Groosham Grange at about the same time. Again, he had believed it was Vincent who had stolen one of his exam papers because Vincent had collected them. But who had he handed them to? Mr Helliwell. With his voodoo powers, it would have been easy for the teacher to animate the waxworks and, of course, he had been part of the contest in London from the start. Always Mr Helliwell. He had befriended David's parents at the prize-giving and it had been he who had found Aunt Mildred's lost handbag.

"Are you surprised to see me?" Mr Helliwell asked and smiled. In his ragged black suit, top hat and tails, he looked like some sort of mad scarecrow or perhaps a circus entertainer down on his luck.

"No," David said.

"I never thought you'd escape from the East Tower," the voodoo teacher said. He glanced at the fallen broomstick. "I presume that's Mrs Windergast's," he went on. "You really have been very resourceful, David. Very brave. I'm sorry it's all been for nothing."

He brought his hand up and now David saw

the Unholy Grail nestling in his huge palm. David tried to move but there was nothing he could do. It was just the two of them and the Unholy Grail. The cathedral had shut for the evening and the close itself was empty. The sun was creeping down towards the horizon and the whole building was shining with a soft, golden light. But the shadows were still sharp. The shadow from the third, single spire was as clear as ever, edging closer towards him as the sun set. All Mr Helliwell had to do was hold out his arm. The Unholy Grail would pass into the shadow of Canterbury Cathedral. Groosham Grange would fall.

"It's the end, David," Mr Helliwell said, his voice low and almost sad. "In a way, I'm glad you're here to see it. Of course, once I pass the Grail into the shadow, you'll crumble into dust. But I always liked you. I want you to know that."

"Thanks," David muttered through gritted teeth.

"Well. I suppose we'd better get it over with." The hand holding the Grail moved slowly. The Grail passed through the last of the sunlight.

"Wait!" David shouted. "There's one thing I want to know!"

Mr Helliwell hesitated. The Grail glittered in his hand only centimetres from the shadow of

319

the cathedral.

"You've got to tell me," David said. He tried to stand but his legs were still too weak. "Why did you do it?"

Mr Helliwell considered. He looked up at the sky. "There's still thirty minutes' sunlight," he said. "If you think you can trick me, boy..."

"No, no." David shook his head. Even that hurt him. "You're far too clever for me, Mr Helliwell. I admit it. But I've a right to know. Why did you set me up? Why did Vincent have to win the Unholy Grail?"

"All right." Mr Helliwell relaxed, lowering the Grail. But the shadow stayed there, hungry, inching ever closer.

"When I started making my plans, I didn't care who won the Unholy Grail," Mr Helliwell began. "But then I happened to see that letter from your father." David remembered. He had dropped it in the corridor, after the fight with Vincent. Mr Helliwell had picked it up. "When I saw that your parents were coming to the prize-giving and then going on to Margate, it was too good an opportunity to miss. Somehow I'd slip it into their luggage and they'd carry it off for me. Nobody would suspect.

"But then I realized that I couldn't let you win it, David. If you had the Grail and then it disappeared, your parents would have been stopped before they got anywhere near the jetty. People would assume you'd given it to them. But Vincent was perfect. He had no parents, no relatives. While everyone was looking for him, nobody would be looking for you or for anyone connected with you."

"So you sent the waxworks."

"Yes. I followed you to London. I was always there."

"But there's still one thing you haven't told me." The pain in David's shoulder and leg was getting worse. He wondered if he could stop himself from passing out. At the same time, his mind was racing. Was he completely helpless? Did he have any power left? "Why did you do it, Mr Helliwell?" he asked. "Why?"

The teacher laughed, a booming hollow laugh tinged with malice. "I know what you're thinking," he said. "You really believe you can catch me off guard?" Mr Helliwell reached out with his foot and pushed David back down on to the grass. David cried out and the world swam in front of his eyes but still he forced himself to stay conscious. "You are searching for magic, boy. But you have none. We've talked enough. It's time for you to join the dust of the earth..."

The Grail came up again.

"Why did you do it?" David shouted. "You were the best. One of the great voodoo magicians.

You couldn't have faked that. You were famous..."

"I was converted!" Mr Helliwell snapped out the three words and even as he spoke them a strange light came into his eyes. "An English missionary – the Bishop of Bletchley – came to Haiti and I met him. My first thought was to turn him into a toad or a snake or a watermelon. But then we got talking. We talked for hours. And he showed me the error of my ways."

"What do you mean?"

"All my life I had been evil, child. Like you. Like everyone at Groosham Grange. He persuaded me that it was time to do good. To crush the school and to kill everybody in it."

"That doesn't sound very good to me," David remarked. "Crushing and killing! What had we ever done to you?"

"You were evil!"

"That's nonsense!" And even as David began to speak he at last understood what Mr Fitch and Mr Teagle had been trying to tell him. The difference between good and evil.

"Groosham Grange isn't evil," he went on. "It's just different – that's all. Monsieur Leloup may be a werewolf and Mr Kilgraw may be a vampire but that's not their fault. They were born that way. And what about Mr Creer? Just because he's a ghost, it doesn't mean he hasn't got a right to be left in peace!"

"Evil!" Mr Helliwell insisted.

"Look who's talking!" David replied. "You're the one who's been lying and cheating. You're the one who pushed me out of the tower – and when that didn't work, you tied me up and left me to die. You stole the Unholy Grail – my parents have probably been disintegrated by now – and you've also destroyed half of Margate. You may think you're some sort of saint, Mr Helliwell, but the truth is you probably did less damage when you were a fully-fledged black magician back on Haiti!"

"You don't know what you're saying, boy…" Mr Helliwell's face had grown pale and there was a dull red flicker in his eyes. "I did what I did for the good of mankind."

"It doesn't matter why you did it or who you did it for," David insisted. "It's easy enough to say that, isn't it? But when you stop and think about what you're doing … that's different. You're crushing and killing. You said it yourself. And I don't think that makes you a saint, Mr Helliwell. I think it makes you a monster and a fanatic."

"I … I … I…" Mr Helliwell was beside himself with rage. His eyes were bulging and one corner of his mouth twitched. He tried to speak but only saliva flecked over his lips. "Enough!"

he hissed. "I've listened to enough!"

Mr Helliwell raised the Unholy Grail. For a moment it caught the sun, magnifying it and splintering it into a dazzling ball of red light. The shadow cast by the one, solitary spire reached out for the Grail.

And David pushed.

In the last few seconds he had formed a plan and had stored up all his remaining strength to make it work. He had argued with the teacher to keep him busy, to divert his attention from what was about to happen. *Because as long as the Unholy Grail was out of the shadow, some power remained.* David used that power now. Guided by him, Mrs Windergast's broomstick suddenly leapt off the grass and hurtled, faster than a bullet, towards Mr Helliwell's head.

The teacher ducked. The broomstick whipped over his shoulder and continued its journey up.

"Missed!" Mr Helliwell threw back his head and laughed. "So that was what you were trying? Well, it didn't work, David. And so ... goodbye!"

With a malevolent smile, he jerked his arm out, thrusting the Unholy Grail into the shadow of Canterbury Cathedral.

But the shadow was no longer there.

Mr Helliwell frowned and looked down at

the grass. The sun was shining, uninterrupted by the spire.

"What...?" he began.

He looked up.

When David had sent the broomstick on its final journey, he hadn't been aiming at the voodoo teacher. Its flight had continued, over the man's head and up into the air, towards the cathedral. It had found its target in the church spire and, strengthened by David's magic, the wooden handle had passed clean through the stone, slicing it in half. The top of the spire had been cut off. The sun had been allowed through. The Unholy Grail was still protected by its light.

"You...!" Mr Helliwell growled.

He never finished the sentence. The broomstick had sliced through a tonne of stone. The top of the spire, a massive chunk that tapered to a point, crashed down.

It landed on Mr Helliwell.

David couldn't look. He heard a single, high-pitched scream, then a sickening thud. Something fell on to the grass, next to his hand. He reached out and took it. It was the Unholy Grail.

Moving slowly, David forced himself up on to his feet and staggered away from the rubble, taking the Grail with him. Every movement hurt him. After every step he had to stop and catch his breath. But soon he was away from the shadow of Canterbury Cathedral and, pressing the Grail against his chest, he continued on through the safety of the dying evening light.

DEPARTURE

The waves rolled in towards Skrull Island, glittering in the morning sun, then broke – silver – on the slanting rocks. A gentle breeze wafted over the shoreline, tracing patterns in the sand. Everything was peaceful. Butterflies danced in the warm sunshine and the air was filled with the scent of flowers.

It was actually the first week of December and the rest of England was covered by snow, with biting winds and cloudy skies. But the magic had returned to Groosham Grange along with the Unholy Grail. And after all the excitement, Mr Fitch and Mr Teagle had decided to give everyone three weeks' extra summer sun as a reward.

The school had been quickly restored. The moment the Grail had been put back in its right place, Groosham Grange had risen out of the rubble as proud and as strong as it had been before. Indeed, there were even a few improvements. Several of the classrooms had repainted themselves in the process and a new computer wing had mysteriously risen out of the swampland that lay to the west of the cemetery.

The staff had also been busy. It had taken a long and complicated spell to repair all the damage that had been done to both Margate and to Canterbury Cathedral, but they had managed it. Then they had made everyone involved – from the waiters and waitresses at the Snappy Eater to the police and ordinary citizens – forget everything that had happened. The Eliots and Aunt Mildred had been restored and returned home. It was small wonder that the entire school was in need of a holiday.

Two months had passed since David's flight to Canterbury. He was sitting now in Mr Kilgraw's darkened study, one leg in plaster, his face still bruised and pale. The assistant headmaster was sitting opposite him. "So have you come to a decision?" he asked.

"Yes, sir," David said. "I've decided I want to leave the school."

Mr Kilgraw nodded but said nothing. A chink of sunlight spilled through a crack in the curtain and he glanced at it distastefully. "May I ask why?" he said.

David thought for a moment. It seemed to him that he had been thinking about what he was going to say for weeks. But now that it was time to put it into words, he wasn't so sure. "I do like it here," he said. "I've been very happy. But..." He drew a breath. "I just think I've had enough magic. I feel I've learned everything I want to learn and now it's time to go back into the real world."

"To learn about life."

"Yes. I suppose so. And anyway..." This was the difficult part. "When I look back at what happened with Vincent and everything, I still think I was to blame. The truth is, I really wanted the Unholy Grail. I wanted it more than anything I've ever wanted in my life and that made me behave ... badly." He broke off. The words sounded so feeble somehow. "I'm worried about how I behaved," he concluded. "And so I think it's time to go."

"Maybe you want to learn more about yourself," Mr Kilgraw said.

"I suppose so."

The assistant headmaster stood up and to David's surprise he was smiling. "You're a very remarkable young man," he said. "Our top student. The rightful winner of the Unholy Grail. And you're right. We've taught you everything you need to know. We already knew that. Why do you think we allowed all this to happen?"

It took David a few seconds to play back what Mr Kilgraw had just said and understand the meaning. "You knew about Mr Helliwell!" he stammered.

"We knew more than perhaps we pretended. But, you see, we had to be sure that you were ready. Think of it as one final test. Before your departure."

"But..." David's mind was reeling. "The Grail! Canterbury Cathedral! He came so close..."

The smile on Mr Kilgraw's face broadened. "We had complete faith in you, David. We knew you wouldn't let us down."

He went over to the door and opened it. David stood up, supporting himself on a stick. "Where do you think you'll go?" Mr Kilgraw asked.

"Well, I'm not going home, if that's what you mean," David said. "I thought I'd see a bit of the world. Mrs Windergast says that Tibet is very interesting at this time of the year..."

"You'll fly?"

"Yes." Now it was David's turn to smile. "But not on a plane."

Mr Kilgraw held out a hand. "Good luck," he said. "And remember, we'll always be here if you need us. Make sure you keep in touch."

They shook hands. David left the study and went back outside. One of the junior classes was out on the lawn – or rather, as they were practising levitation, just above it. Gregor, who had been trying to get a suntan, was sitting in a deckchair, his body gently smoking. The sun was still high in the sky. David followed the path over to the top of the cliffs. His favourite place on the island.

Vincent and Jill were waiting for him, sitting together, looking at the waves.

"Did you tell him?" Jill asked, as he arrived.

"Yes."

"What did he say?"

"He wished me luck."

"You'll probably need it," Vincent said. "I'm sorry you're going, David. I'll really miss you."

"I'll miss you too, Vincent. And you, Jill. In fact I'll even miss Gregor. But I expect we'll meet again. Somehow I don't think I've heard the last of Groosham Grange."

Vincent nodded and stood up. Jill took David's arm. And together the three friends walked down towards the sea.

STORMBREAKER
Anthony Horowitz

Meet Alex Rider, the reluctant teenage spy.

When his guardian dies in suspicious circumstances, fourteen-year-old Alex Rider finds his world turned upside down.

Within days he's gone from schoolboy to superspy. Forcibly recruited into MI6, Alex has to take part in gruelling SAS training exercises. Then, armed with his own special set of secret gadgets, he's off on his first mission.

His destination is the depths of Cornwall, where Middle Eastern multimillionaire Herod Sayle is producing his state-of-the-art Stormbreaker computers. Sayle's offered to give one free to every school in the country – but MI6 think there's more to the gift than meets the eye.

Only Alex can find out the truth. But time is running out and Alex soon finds himself in mortal danger. It looks as if his first assignment may well be his last...

Explosive, thrilling, action-packed, *Stormbreaker* reveals Anthony Horowitz at his brilliant best.

"Is there anybody in Britain who will not enjoy this fabulous junior James Bond adventure?"
The Daily Mail

"The perfect hero ... genuine 21st-century stuff."
The Daily Telegraph

POINT BLANC
Anthony Horowitz

Alex Rider, teenage superspy, is back!

Fourteen-year-old Alex Rider, reluctant MI6 spy, is back at school trying to adapt to his new double life ... and to double homework.

But MI6 have other plans for him.

Investigations into the "accidental" deaths of two of the world's most powerful men have revealed just one link. Both had a son attending Point Blanc Academy – an exclusive school for rebellious rich kids, run by the sinister Dr Grief and set high on an isolated mountain peak in the French Alps.

Armed only with a false ID and a new collection of brilliantly disguised gadgets, Alex must infiltrate the academy as a pupil and establish the truth about what is really happening there. Can he alert the world to what he discovers before it is too late?

"Horowitz will grip you with suspense, daring and cheek – and that's just the first page! Prepare for action scenes as fast as a movie. A stormin' follow-up to *Stormbreaker*." *The Times*

"A hugely entertaining, fast-paced book which more than deserves five stars."
www.cool-reads.co.uk